PREGNANT WITH A ROYAL BABY!

BY
SUSAN MEIER

MILLS & BOON

All rights reserved including the right of reproduction in whole or in part in any form. This edition is published by arrangement with Harlequin Books S.A.

This is a work of fiction. Names, characters, places, locations and incidents are purely fictional and bear no relationship to any real life individuals, living or dead, or to any actual places, business establishments, locations, events or incidents. Any resemblance is entirely coincidental.

First published in Great Britain 2016
By Mills & Boon, an imprint of HarperCollins*Publishers*
1 London Bridge Street, London, SE1 9GF

© 2016 Linda Susan Meier

ISBN: 978-0-263-26361-9

Our policy is to use papers that are natural, renewable and recyclable products and made from wood grown in sustainable forests. The logging and manufacturing processes conform to the legal environmental regulations of the country of origin.

Printed and bound in Great Britain
by CPI Antony Rowe, Chippenham, Wiltshire

Susan Meier is the author of over fifty books for Mills & Boon. *The Tycoon's Secret Daughter* was a RITA® Award finalist, and *Nanny for the Millionaire's Twins* won the Book Buyer's Best award and was a finalist in the National Reader's Choice awards. She is married and has three children. One of eleven children, she loves to write about the complexity of families and totally believes in the power of love.

Books by Susan Meier

Mills & Boon Romance

The Vineyards of Calanetti
A Bride for the Italian Boss

Mothers in a Million
A Father for Her Triplets

The Larkville Legacy
The Billionaire's Baby SOS

First Time Dads!
The Tycoon's Secret Daughter
Nanny for the Millionaire's Twins

Kisses on Her Christmas List
Single Dad's Christmas Miracle
Daring to Trust the Boss
The Twelve Dates of Christmas
Her Brooding Italian Boss

Visit the Author Profile page at millsandboon.co.uk for more titles.

To my own Prince Charming, and our marriage—
a journey of ups and downs that surprises me
every day. Usually in a good way. :)

CHAPTER ONE

WHEN THE DOORBELL to her condo rang, Virginia Jones, Ginny for short, had just gotten out of the shower after a long, long day at Jefferson High School in Terra Mas, Texas. Her school was the last on a list of places Prince Dominic Sancho of Xaviera, a small island country between Spain and Algeria, was visiting on a good-will tour. As guidance counselor, she'd shown him the school and introduced him to staff, then herded the kids into the gymnasium, where he'd given an hour-long talk on global economics: how the world was a much smaller place than it had been before the internet.

She'd loved the talk, but she'd liked looking at Prince Dominic even more. Tall and broad shouldered, he filled out the formal uniform of his royalty like a man meant to be a king. His dark eyes sparkled with amusement at the antics of "her" kids. His full lips had never stopped smiling.

If it were permitted for grown women to swoon, she would have made a fool of herself with him that afternoon. As it was, common sense had kept her professional. And now she was tired. Not up for a visitor.

Her doorbell rang again.

She gave her glass of wine a longing look before she rose from her sofa.

"I'm coming." She said it just as she reached the door. Going up on tiptoes, she peeked through the peephole. When she saw Prince Dominic, she gasped and jumped back.

Her doorbell rang again.

She peered down at her sweatpants and tank top, ran a hand along her still-wet long blond hair and knew this would go down in the annals of her life as one of her most embarrassing moments.

With no choice, she pasted a smile on her face and opened the door.

He laughed. "I caught you at a bad time."

"Unfortunately." Just looking at him made her heart speed up. He'd removed the royal uniform and replaced it with a lightweight white V-neck sweater and jeans. Not a hair of his shiny black curls was out of place. His dark eyes sparkled with amusement.

"You probably think all Americans are idiots."

"No, I think the United States is a very comfortable country." He paused long enough to lift his perfect lips into a warm smile. "Are you going to invite me in?"

She motioned for him to come in with a wave of her hand and kept hyperventilation at bay only by a miracle of self-discipline. She had a *prince* entering her house. A good-looking, good-natured, good *everything* prince.

As she closed the door, he said, "I'd actually come here tonight to see if you'd like to have dinner with me." He shrugged. "And show me your town."

She had to work to keep her eyes from bugging. He wanted to take her *out*? Then she realized his request made sense. She'd shown him the school. Of course, she was the prime candidate to show him the town. He was not asking her out.

"Then I thought maybe we'd fly to Los Angeles and go to a club."

She let her eyes bulge. Okay. He *was* asking her out. "You want to go clubbing?"

"Don't you like to dance?"

Her heart tripped over itself in her chest. "I love to dance."

He smiled. "Me, too. I'm afraid I don't get to dance often, though. Duty supersedes fun. Please say you'll come with me."

"I'd love to."

Though he was in jeans, he looked good enough to eat, so she slithered into her prettiest red party dress, put on her best makeup and slid into tall black sandals.

They had dinner at the local Italian restaurant, with his bodyguards unobtrusively eating at the tables beside theirs, then they actually got on his royal jet and flew to LA, where they'd danced until three. He should have dropped her off at her building lobby. Instead, he came up to her condo, and the few kisses they'd shared in his limo turned into passionate lovemaking. The best sex of her life. She'd kissed him goodbye at the door in her one and only fancy robe—which she'd retrieved from her closet when he made the call to his driver that he was ready. Then just when she was about to shower for school again, he called her.

"Thank you."

The sweetness of his words caused her throat to tighten. Her voice was soft and breathless when she said, "You're welcome."

"I'm sorry we'll never meet again."

"Me, too."

But in a way she wasn't. She'd had a wonderful fairy-tale night with a prince, something she could hold in her heart forever. There would be no need to worry if he would be a good king or a bad king; no need to know if he did stupid things like hog the bathroom; no need to worry if the stress of his job would make him an alcoholic, as her dad had been. No need to know the real Prince Dominic Sancho.

There had been one glorious, wonderful night. No regrets and no worries about the future. The way she liked all her relationships.

They hung up on mutual sighs. In the process of setting her phone on her bedside table, she realized that because he'd called her, she had his number. She clicked a few buttons and when the digits came up caller ID said private line. She smiled. She didn't just have his number she had his *private* number.

That pleased her enormously. If she ever got curious or lonely, she could call him…

Or not. Best to sit and stare at his number and imagine good things. Not bad. Never bad. She'd had enough bad in her life.

Knowing there was no time to sleep, she dressed for school, hugging her secret to herself. For two weeks she walked on a cloud of happiness, then one morning she woke and realized she hadn't gotten her period, and she knew there *really* was a good reason to have his private number.

"Thank God our country isn't like Britain used to be where the future king had to marry a virgin."

Prince Dominic Sancho held back the anger that threatened to rise up in him. He'd been the perfect royal for nearly thirty years and one slip, one reckless night in America, had wiped all that away. His father might be angry, but it was *his* life plan that had been changed.

In order to ensure the integrity of the line and the safety of his child, he had no choice but to marry Ginny Jones, a woman he didn't know.

"Yes. Thank God I'm permitted to marry the mother of my child."

"I was being facetious." Short and bald, with a round belly, his father, the king of Xaviera, was an imposing, strict man. He hated mistakes. Couldn't even tolerate slipups. Especially not from the son who was his successor.

"And I was being sarcastic." It wasn't often that he got smart with his father. In fact, he probably hadn't done it more than five times in his entire life, including his teen years. But discovering a simple one-night stand had resulted in a pregnancy had pushed him over the edge. His brother was the king of playboys but did he ever suffer a consequence for his actions? No. Yet the first time Dom stepped out of line, he was punished.

"I've arranged for you and Ms. Jones to meet with the protocol officials whenever you're ready. But no later than tomorrow morning." King Ronaldo caught his gaze. "Prepare your *bride*."

The insult in his father's voice cut through Dom like a knife. He just barely succeeded in not sniping back.

He rose from his seat across from the ornate desk that was the seat of power for the king. He should have said, "Thank you for your time, Your Majesty." A good prince would have done that. Instead he said, "I'll get back to you."

"See to it that this wedding is done right. I will not be so easy on you if you screw up again."

He bowed and headed out of the room. *I will not be so easy on you if you screw up again?*

Anger coursed through him. He stifled it. His father

was the king. Dominic was heir to the throne. He *knew* there were protocols and rules. He'd broken them. He deserved this.

Still…the penalty for one misstep was marriage? *Marriage.*

After the way his father had fallen apart when his mother died, Dominic understood why his dad was careful, rigid now. His grief had been so intense that he hadn't come out of his quarters for six weeks and in that time the country had begun to crumble. Parliament nearly took his crown, and, watching it all unfold, Dominic had promised himself he would never marry, never soften so much that a loss nearly destroyed him.

When an opportunity for a treaty had arisen, the price being his marriage to a princess of a country that had been an enemy for centuries, he'd thought why not? Not only was the feud between their kingdoms old enough that it was time to retire it, but also there'd be no real emotional ties in a marriage that was part of a treaty, and he'd get an heir who would be a prince in two countries. But now here he was. Forced to marry a woman he didn't know, ruining his design for a double royal heir, because of his own carelessness.

His life plan really had gone to hell.

He sucked in a breath and walked to the back stairway that led to his private quarters, buying time before he had to talk to Ginny. If he was angry, he couldn't imagine how she felt—

Unless she'd gotten pregnant deliberately?

The horribleness of the thought froze his blood, stopped his breathing, and he told himself to calm down. Too many things had to align for her to have orchestrated the pregnancy, including the fact that he was the one who had gone to her condo that night. And she'd been a cute mess. Wet hair. Sweatpants. She obviously hadn't been planning on seeing him that night.

Reaching the top floor of the east wing of Xaviera's palace, he strode in the direction of the white double doors with intricate scroll designs carved down the sides. The huge square "waiting" area between the top of the stairs and his apartment had scant furnishings, though the walls were adorned with art. Picasso. Rembrandt. Monet. Hidden treasures. Mostly for his viewing. Because that's what his life was. Special. Honored. In spite of the awkward meeting with his father, he knew that he was different. Some day he would be a king.

The click of his heels echoed as he walked along the marble floor. When he reached the doors, he took both handles and opened them onto his home, his haven.

Virginia Jones rose from the tufted bench seat in what served as a foyer for his apartment. Medium height, with long yellow hair and the kind of body that tempts a man to do exactly what he had done the night he met her, Ginny was every man's fantasy. When her striking blue eyes met his, he remembered how adorable she was at the Texas high school, a guidance counselor beloved by her students. He also remembered the hot little red dress she'd slipped into when he'd persuaded her to go clubbing with him. The dress had brought out the best of her figure, almost made him drool and turned him into a real live Prince Charming. Seducing her had been second nature. The sex had been amazing.

It seemed that was all he could think about when he looked at her. And now he was about to make her a princess.

"So?"

"So, my father and my kingdom wish for us to marry."

Those bright blue eyes met his. "Wish?"

He motioned for her to follow him into his formal living room. More marble floors greeted them, except these were covered by rich red Oriental rugs. White sofas flanked a white marble fireplace. Red pillows gave the room some color. He gestured for Virginia to take a seat while he strode to the bar and grabbed the decanter of Scotch.

"Can I get you a drink?"

She gaped at him. "I'm pregnant."

He winced. "Right." He took a breath. "How about some orange juice?"

"I'm fine." She held his gaze. "I'm more anxious to learn my fate than to pretend we're having a tea party."

He had no idea where the attitude had come from, but that was the truth of getting intimate with someone you didn't know. She could be the Wicked Witch of the West, or a woman who wanted to save the whales, or a woman who had no loyalties at all, a woman who was lazy, crass or stupid, and he was stuck with her.

"All right." He walked to the sofa across from the one on which she sat and set his Scotch on the glass table between them. "Maybe the better way to put it is that they are *requesting* that we marry."

"So I have a choice?"

"Not really. You are pregnant with the heir to Xaviera's throne. If you decide not to marry me, your child will be taken from you."

She gasped. "What?"

"He or she is the heir to our throne. There isn't a country in the world who'd dare supersede our laws with their own when it comes to royalty, especially royalty in line to rule the country."

She bounced from her seat. "That's not fair!"

He sat back, watching her long legs as she paced. Though she wore jeans and a snug sweater, he pictured those legs beneath the shiny red dress. "Try suing. Waste time. Ruin the chance for us to have a royal wedding. Ruin the chance for the gossip to die down and our child to be brought into the world with a celebration instead of whispers."

She stopped pacing and caught his gaze, obviously thinking through what he'd said.

He took advantage of her weak moment. "You won't win and you'll bring our child into a world of chaos for nothing because I have a plan."

"A plan?"

Ginny stared at the gorgeous man on the sofa. With eyes so dark they almost looked black and onyx hair, he was every inch a prince. A royal. A future ruler who lived a life of privilege. A man just a little bit above everybody else.

As they talked about a situation that would totally change her life, he very calmly sipped Scotch.

"My father wants the next king to be born in wedlock." He held her gaze. "Our subjects will, too. But that doesn't mean we have to stay married."

Relieved, she sat on the sofa across from him again. "It doesn't?"

"No. But it does mean we have to play a part for a while." He glanced at his Scotch then back up at her. "Over the next couple of days, as the protocol office begins planning our wedding, we'll be seen together in public."

Her heart thumped when he said *wedding*. She would be married to a guy who would someday be a king. Did that mean sleeping with him? They might be at odds now, but the night they'd gone out, they'd had a really good time. She had no idea how *that* factored into his plan, so she kept her face calm, simply kept her gaze locked with his, hoping to appear cooler than she was.

"Next week we'll announce our engagement, quick wedding and pregnancy all at once."

That didn't sound fun. "Oh, boy."

"Don't worry. I've thought this through. The people of Xaviera will be thrilled to see me getting married. But the only thing they love better than a royal wedding is a royal pregnancy. If we play this right, the next few months could be a wonderful time for the people of my kingdom."

"Okay." Her nerves popped and jumped, but she resisted the urge to bounce off the sofa and pace again. If he could be calm, she could be calm. And really what he said made sense. They were doing this for his people and their child, a future king, who deserved to be born amid celebration.

"So we'd get married next month and after that we'd spend the rest of your pregnancy making appearances as the happy couple expecting the next heir to the throne, then the baby will be born to a country excited and happy about his birth."

She could picture it. She'd seen enough of Britain's royal family's weddings, as well as their pregnancies, to have a pretty good idea of what she was in for. Except Xaviera was a small country, much smaller than Britain, so she could probably cut the exposure in the press and even in Xaviera itself in about half. Which wouldn't be *too* bad.

"After that we should stay married until the baby's about two. At age two, there's a ceremony that would induct him or her into the line of reigning Sanchos. We can be cool to each other at that ceremony, and then we can divorce without causing too much of a stir because after that nothing press worthy happens in his life until he turns twelve." He sat back. "If people want to say we married hastily, or even if they say we only married for the baby, we agree. But waiting until he or she is two shows we gave the marriage a good shot. Because we'll be fair and calm about it, everyone will support us."

"And what about the baby?"

"What about the baby?"

"Who keeps him? What kind of custody arrangements are we talking about here?"

"There are a few scenarios. I was hoping you'd let the years we're married go by without making any final decisions, but if you choose to take our child back to America, a contingent of bodyguards will be sent with you. Xaviera will purchase a home with suitable security."

"What about my job?"

"Your job will be mother to Xaviera's heir. At least until he or she is twelve."

"Twelve?"

"Up until twelve he can be homeschooled. After that there are mandatory boarding schools. He or she has to have a certain kind of education."

"No public school, huh?"

"Mock if you want, but that is the situation." He rose from the sofa. "Once he goes to boarding school, your life is your own again. Except you will be expected to attend all of his public functions."

She could see it. She could picture herself as the future king's mom, wiping grape jelly from her little boy's chin in private, and way, way out of the view of cameras when he was in public. Knowing that she'd easily slip out of the limelight settled some of her nerves. Still, there was more to it than grape jelly and hiding from cameras.

"I'll give you a week to think about it."

"A week?"

"The week you're at the palace. The time we're getting out. Being seen in public. Having a date or two."

Their eyes met. Their last date had been fantastic. But it was also what had gotten them into this mess.

"I think I still have some more questions."

"About the dates?"

She nodded.

"Like, will we kiss?"

A starburst of tingles exploded in her stomach. She nodded again.

"Yes. We have to pretend we adore each other. That we met and swept each other off our respective feet." He held her gaze. "Which we sort of did."

Memories of holding hands, intimate touches and those unbelievable kisses rippled through her, tightening her chest, sending her pulse into overdrive.

"But sex is off the table." He smiled. "Unless you're interested."

Her heart thumped. She tried to imagine herself resisting that smile, that charm—

Actually, he hadn't been all that charming in this chat, except when it suited him. That was the curse of getting involved with someone she didn't know. She'd met and made love with Prince Charming. She had no idea who the real Prince Dominic was. What if he was like her dad? Only pulling out the charm to get what he wanted?

Oh. No brainer. She could resist that like sour wine at a bad dance club.

"Ginny, this relationship can go any way you want."

And the stoic, respectable prince was back. "Behind the walls of this palace we can be as distant or as intimate as you wish. But make no mistake. If you marry me, it's temporary. Don't get stars in your eyes. Don't get any big ideas. This marriage will not become permanent. I had been promised to a princess as part of a treaty and that was what I wanted. A marriage that meant something, accomplished something. A real marriage doesn't work in my world. So this little arrangement will not turn permanent. You need to know that, too, before you decide."

CHAPTER TWO

"So it will be totally a marriage of convenience?"

Ginny lay on the bed in the suite across the great room in Dominic's palace apartment. Cool silk caressed her back. Fluffy pillows supported her. Rich aqua walls brought color and life to the cavernous space.

"That's it. Nothing but a marriage of convenience to bring the heir to Xaviera's throne into the world legitimately."

"Oh, sweetie, that's weird."

"I know, Mom. But you have to remember the child we created will be in the public eye his entire life. How selfish would it be for me to refuse to marry Dominic, and have the heir to Xavier's throne born in a way that causes whispers and gossip that follow him forever?"

"True."

"Besides, this might just be the best thing for me, too. I mean, seriously, I don't know Dominic. What he said today about not wanting to be married proves it. He was such a sweetheart when he came to the school that day that I thought he really was a Prince Charming."

"They're all Prince Charming on dates, Ginny. It's real life that brings out their bad side."

Ginny winced. Though Dominic and her alcoholic dad seemed to share the charm gene, her dad had been mean and emotionally abusive. Dominic just seemed formal. It wasn't fair to compare the two—even if she would be wise about the charm part.

"He's not a bad guy, Mom. He's just not the happy-go-lucky guy he was on our date. And, you know what? I'm probably not the starry-eyed, flirty girl I was that night, either. We were both just having fun. But this pregnancy is real. And that's why he's serious."

"Okay. You're right."

"I know I'm right, but I still don't know what to do."

"It sounds like you think you should marry him. What are you giving up? A year, a year and a half of your life?"

"About two and a half years, and my career. Apparently, my job for the next twelve years is to be the heir's mom."

Ginny's mom laughed. "Even if your child wasn't a prince or princess, your priorities would switch from your job to this baby." She sucked in a breath. "You know what? This isn't all that much different from having the baby of a commoner."

"Except for dealing with the press."

"Yeah, well, the press is different."

"And boarding school."

"There is that."

"And living in a palace."

"Right, palace." Her mother sighed. "But the situation is done, Ginny."

"I suppose."

"So what concerns you?"

"Well, I have to see if I can handle it. Dominic's given me a week to make up my mind. He said we'd go out in public a few times." She groaned. "Oh, damn."

"What?"

"I brought jeans and T-shirts. One sundress." She dropped her head to her hands. "I'm going to go out with a prince, in public, in my junky clothes?"

"Your wardrobe is fine. *You'll* be fine."

"Right." She hadn't even told her mom about kissing Dom, possibly sleeping with Dom. All she'd mentioned was not knowing Dominic and changing her life to suit a baby, and just that had scared her silly.

This was a mess.

Two quick knocks at her door brought her head off the pillow. "Yes?"

"It's me. Dominic. My father requests our presence at dinner tonight."

Ginny turned toward the wall and whispered, "Gotta go, Mom," into the phone before she rolled off the bed and said, "Sure. That's fine. What time?"

"Seven." He cleared his throat. "It's semiformal."

She gaped at the door, as discomfort swamped her. Not only did she not have a semiformal dress for dinner, but her suite had a private sitting room outside her bedroom. He had to be in that room to be knocking on her bedroom door. He might have knocked on the door to her suite before inviting himself in, but she wouldn't have heard him. The darned place was so big and had such high ceilings that sound either echoed or disappeared. He wasn't infringing on her privacy. She hoped.

"Semiformal?"

"I took the liberty of having the staff get some suitable clothes for you."

Pride almost caused her to say, "I'm fine." But when she looked down at her jeans and considered the contents of her suitcase, she knew this was the first step in many toward giving up her real life.

"You're right. I have nothing acceptable to meet a

king." She walked to the door, opened it and watched as four men brought in bags and boxes and armloads of dresses, including gowns.

"Oh, my God."

Dominic walked in behind the parade of men. "Even if you decide not to marry me, you're here for a week."

Her mouth fell open at the ease with which he spoke in front of staff, but the expression of not a single man even twitched. This was one well-trained staff.

She took a quick breath. "So I need to be semiformal."

He nodded. "Yes."

"Okay. Scram. I have some work to do to be presentable."

"I can have a hairdresser sent up. Manicurist. Masseuse."

"Why would I need a massage?"

"Maybe what I should get you is a rundown on my dad. Then you'd very clearly understand why you want to be Zen and you'd get the massage."

"Great."

She took advantage of the hairdresser and manicurist, and ten minutes before it was time to leave for dinner she wished she'd agreed to the masseuse.

Dressed in a lightweight blue dress that stopped midcalf, with her hair in an updo suitable for a woman of seventy and old-fashioned pumps dyed to match the dress, she stepped out of her bedroom.

Standing in the great room, Dominic smiled. Unlike her ugly blue dress, his tux appeared to have been made for him. Again he was every inch a prince. Handsome. Debonair. Regal.

While she looked like a frumpy old bat.

"You look lovely."

"I look like the Queen of England. Get me a hat and one of those sedate purses she carries all the time and people would probably get us confused."

He laughed. "You are meeting a king."

"Who wants to be reminded of his grandmother?"

"You do not look like a grandmother."

"Well, I sure as hell don't look like a twenty-five-year-old guidance counselor in the coolest school in Texas."

"Trust me. You will want the armor of a grandma dress when you meet my dad." He took her elbow and led her to the door, out of the apartment and through the echoing lobby to the waiting elevator.

As they stepped inside and the door closed behind them, she said, "You have some impressive art."

"We are royalty."

"I guess I'd better get used to that." That and ugly clothes.

"That's why we're giving you the week. To get accustomed to us."

She released her breath in a slow sigh. She knew that, of course. She also suspected the clothes weren't ugly as much as they were dignified.

"Who picked out these clothes anyway?"

He stared straight ahead at the closed elevator door. "I did."

She pulled the skirt of the too-big dress away from her hips. "Because you think your dad will like me better in baggy clothes?"

"I was a bit off on your size. But it's better to be too big than too small."

"Couldn't you at least have gotten something red?"

"Blue matches your eyes."

The sweetness of that caught her off guard. For a

second she'd forgotten he knew the color of her eyes. But thinking about it, she remembered that gazing into her eyes, making her feel special, had been his seduction superpower.

"Besides, red would have reminded me of that night."

Her lips lifted into a smile. "Oh?"

"You were devastatingly beautiful."

Her heart skipped a beat. He'd made her feel beautiful. "If you hadn't been staring straight ahead when you said that, it would have been romantic."

"We don't want to be romantic, remember?"

"So that means you're not going to look at me?"

"I'm not going to make eye contact. I'm pretty sure that's what got us into trouble on our date."

She laughed, but happiness bubbled inside her. He *liked* her. A *prince* liked her. At the very least, he liked her looks.

It was heady stuff.

The elevator bell rang. The doors opened. Dominic led her out. "The family dining room is this way."

They walked across a short hall to open doors that ushered them into a formal dining room. A table that could have seated forty dominated the space. Four places were set near the head. An older man dressed in a royal uniform and a younger man in a tux like Dominic's rose as they entered.

"Virginia Jones, this is King Ronaldo Sancho and my brother, Prince Alexandros. We call him Alex."

Ginny froze. What was she supposed to do? Curtsy? Bow? Damn it. Why hadn't she paid attention to etiquette—

What etiquette? Guidance counselors knew the basics but nothing else. And she certainly hadn't expected to someday meet a prince, let alone a king. She hadn't attended etiquette classes. Was there even such a thing anymore? She couldn't be mad at herself for not knowing something she'd never been exposed to.

"You hold out your hand," King Ronaldo said irritably. "And it's my choice to kiss it or shake it."

"Oh." She held out her hand. The king shook it.

Great. She'd already blown her first introduction.

Dom turned her in the direction of his brother. As tall as Dominic and every bit as good-looking—though his face had a roundness to it that made him appear kinder, with eyes that sparkled—Alex smiled warmly at her.

"It's a pleasure to meet the woman who snagged my brother."

King Ronaldo growled. "We do not speak that way in this house."

"Really, Father," Alex said, as he took his seat and opened his napkin. "This house is the only place we can speak like that." He smiled at Ginny as Dominic seated her. "It's a pleasure to have you in the family, Ginny, even if my brother does intend to dress you like a grandmother."

With a gasp, she faced Dom. "I told you!"

He almost smiled, but his father let out one of those low growls of disapproval again, and Dominic's face shifted, returning to his formal expression.

As a servant brought in salads, King Ronaldo said, "So, Miss Jones, tell us about yourself."

She swallowed. "Well, you know I'm a guidance counselor at a high school."

"Which is where you met Dominic."

She nodded. "My mother was a teacher. I loved the relationships she had with her students."

Alex said, "So why not teach?"

"I wanted a chance to meet all the kids, know all the kids, not just the ones I was teaching."

The king said, "Ump," but his tone of voice was positive.

She relaxed a bit. But when she glanced at the row of silverware, sweat beaded on her forehead. Seven forks. Just what in the name of all that was holy were they about to eat?

Remembering the rhyme she'd been taught in grade school, she started with the outside fork.

"What else should we know?"

"Actually, Your Majesty, since you've already decided the answer to our problem is to marry, and I'm the one who hasn't made up her mind, I think I should be the one asking questions."

Alex burst out laughing. "I like her."

The king growled again.

Dominic shot her a look of reprimand.

So she smiled and rephrased the question. "It's an honor to have been asked to join your family. But in America we have a saying about not buying a car unless you kick the tires."

Alex laughed again. "Now we're tires."

Not sure if she liked Dominic's brother or not, Ginny shrugged and said, "Or you're the used car. Be glad I didn't use the don't-buy-a-horse-without-checking-its-teeth analogy."

Alex laughed. Dominic groaned. But the king quietly said, "Fair enough. What would you like to know?"

"I don't really have to dress like this for the entire time Dominic and I stay married, do I?"

"You need to look respectable." King Ronaldo inspected her blue dress and grimaced. Even he thought it was ugly. "If we let you choose your own wardrobe, can you do that?"

"Of course, I can do that!"

"You also need to behave with the utmost of decorum in public."

"I can do that, too. Though I might need some help with protocols." She answered honestly, but she hadn't missed the way the king had turned the tables on her again, and she retook control of the conversation. "So what was Dominic like as a child?"

The king said, "Headstrong."

Alex said, "A bully."

Dominic said, "All older brothers bully their baby brothers. It's like a rule."

And for the first time, Ginny felt as if she was actually talking to people. A family.

Alex shook his head. "Do you know he agreed to marry the princess of Grennady when he was only twelve?"

She faced Dom. "Really?"

Their eyes met and memories of holding him close, whispering in his ear, being held and touched and loved by him rolled through her, and she understood why Dominic had been avoiding eye contact in the elevator. Looking into someone's eyes was intimate. In those few seconds, he wasn't just a name or a problem or a memory, he was a real person. The guy she'd made love with. Father of her child.

"My mother had just died. Our kingdom was in a state of mourning from which we couldn't seem to emerge. It was appropriate to do something that didn't just ensure peace—it also brought up morale."

She continued to hold his gaze as he spoke, and something warm and soft floated through her. At twelve, he had been mature enough to do his duty. Hell, he was mature enough to *know* his duty. It was remarkable, amazing.

Alex sighed. "Now I'm stuck marrying her."

She faced Dom's younger brother with a wince. "Really? You have to marry the princess Dom was supposed to marry?"

The king said, "You can't just back out of a twenty-year-old treaty. We promised a marriage. We will deliver a marriage."

Alex batted a hand. "Doesn't matter. The princess and I will have a marriage of convenience." He shrugged. "I'll run around on her. She'll run around on me. Nobody will really know who our babies belong to and we won't allow blood tests. It'll be fine."

The king scowled. "Once again, Alex, I won't have you talk like that at the table."

Silence fell over the foursome. Dominic didn't defend his younger brother, who seemed oddly cowed by the reprimand. Hoping to restart the conversation and shift everybody's attention, Ginny tried to think of a question to ask, but couldn't come up with one to save her soul. She wanted to. She wanted to lift the gloom of talking about a dead queen, mourning subjects and a younger brother resigned to a loveless marriage— his life made tolerable by affairs. But nothing came to mind, except an empty, hollow feeling that *this* was the family she was marrying into.

But even as she thought that, she realized there was a human side to this story. A man had lost his wife and raised two boys alone. One son had become a slave to duty. The other rebellious.

Was the pain of losing a wife and mom any less because they were royal?

In some ways she thought it might have been worse.

Dominic started a conversation about the country's budget and a quiet discussion ensued. When the dinner was over, the king took her hand, bent and kissed it. An apology, she supposed, for the long, difficult dinner. Or maybe an acknowledgment that the next few years of her life would be like this, if she chose to marry Dominic.

They walked back to Dominic's apartment in silence, her blue dress swishing against her calves, mocking her, reminding her just how out of her element she was and just how much she wished she were back at her condo, sitting by the pool, sipping something fruity.

When they entered Dom's apartment, he said, "We'll meet the minister of protocol tomorrow morning."

"Okay." She headed for the double doors of her bedroom suite. "Great."

"Don't let my family scare you."

She stopped, turned to face him. "I'm not afraid of you." She almost said, "I feel sorry for you." For as difficult as the beginning of her life had been, she'd redeemed it. She'd built a world of friends and meaning. Dominic, his brother and the grouchy king were stuck.

But the strange look in his eyes kept her from saying that. He didn't seem embarrassed by his family as much as he appeared interested in what she thought of them. He wanted her to like them. Or approve of them. Or maybe just accept them.

She walked over to him, her ugly dyed blue pumps clicking on the marble floor, echoing in the silence. "I'm very accustomed to dealing with ornery dads. I was fine. Your father and brother might be a little grouchy or stern or even too flip, but I'd have paid to have family like them."

He sniffed a laugh. "Right."

"I'm serious." She smiled slightly. "Your brother needs a week of time-out in his room to get his act together, or maybe a good friend to talk through his life. Your dad lost his wife and lived his grief in the public eye. And you just want to live up to what your dad wants. You're actually a very normal family." Something she'd longed for her entire life. Something that could suck her in if she wasn't careful. "Good night."

As she turned to walk back to her bedroom suite, Dominic whispered, "Good night," confused by what she'd said. From what his investigators had dug up, her father was dead. Her mother adored her and she had a billion friends.

So what was that sad note he heard in her voice?

And why the hell would she have wanted *his* family?

He told himself it couldn't matter and walked to his suite, removing his tie. But the next day when she arrived at the table for breakfast, he jumped to his feet, feeling something he couldn't quite identify. He didn't see her in the red dress, dancing provocatively, happily seducing him. He saw a fresh-faced American girl who had something in her past. Something his private investigator hadn't dug up, but something that made her more than accepting of his stiff and formal father, and sometimes-obnoxious playboy brother.

He pulled out the chair beside his. "What would you like to eat?"

"I'd like one of those oranges," she said, pointing at the fruit in the bowl on the buffet behind the table. "And some toast."

"That's it?"

She shrugged. "It's all I'm hungry for."

He rang for a serving girl and made her request for toast and a glass of water. She plucked an orange from the bowl and began to peel it.

"Did you sleep well?"

"Yes."

"You remember we meet with the minister of protocol this morning?"

"Mmm-hmm."

His nerves jangled and he cursed himself. They were entering into a pretend marriage for the sake of their child. It was her prerogative if she didn't want to get too chummy with him.

Still, it didn't seem right not to say anything while they ate breakfast.

"If you decide to stay and marry me, we'll have your mom flown over, not just for the wedding but for the preparations."

"My mom still teaches."

"Oh."

"I'm twenty-five. She had me when she was twenty-five. That makes her fifty." She peeked up from her orange and smiled at him. "Too young to retire."

"You said she likes teaching."

"She loves teaching."

And the conversation died. Frustration rolled through him. As her toast arrived, he tried to think of something to say; nothing came to him.

She pulled one of the many newspapers provided for him from the stack on the end of the table and began reading. Even as he was glad she was a smart woman who appeared to be up on current events and most likely wouldn't embarrass him, he scowled internally, realizing reading the paper was a good way to avoid talking to him.

After breakfast, they walked along tall-ceilinged corridors to the first floor of the palace and the office of the minister of protocol, their footsteps the only sound around them. If a servant caught a peek at Dominic, he or she froze in place and bowed as he passed by. He barely noticed until he caught a sideways glance at Ginny's face and saw it scrunch in confusion.

"I don't like the fuss."

She peeked over. "Excuse me?"

"I don't like the fuss. But respect is part of the deal. To be an effective leader, your subjects must respect you. Trust you to rule well. Bowing is a sign that they trust you."

"Interesting."

Annoyance skittered through him. "It's not 'interesting.' It's true."

"Okay. Maybe I said that wrong. What I should have said was it's interesting that it's true because it gives me a whole different perspective of you as a leader. It helps me to see you as a leader."

It shouldn't have relieved him so much that she agreed. But he told himself it only mattered because he needed for her to respect him, too, for the years they'd be married.

Finally at the back of the building, they took an elevator to the first floor to the working space of the palace.

"Holy cow. This is big."

"It's huge." He pointed to the right. "The king's offices are over there. My offices and my brother's are near his. To the left," he said, motioning toward a long hall, "are the general offices. This is where our ministers and staff work."

* * *

Not able to see the end of the hall, Ginny blinked. It went so far it was almost like looking at an optical illusion.

He smiled. "I know. Impressive."

She said, "Right." But when her gaze swung around to his, she was no longer talking about the size of the palace. Everything about being royalty was bigger, better, grander than anything she'd ever seen or experienced. The truth of being a commoner washed through her again. His family might have normal bickering siblings with a traditional disciplinarian dad, but she couldn't forget they were rulers. Rich, powerful. The kind of family she shouldn't even cross paths with, let alone marry into.

"This way."

He took her elbow to guide her and sparkly little pinpricks skittered up her arm. She didn't know which was worse—being incredibly attracted to him or her good reaction to his brother and dad. Either one of them could get her into trouble. She shouldn't have admitted the night before that she'd have loved to have had a family like his. She could see it had made him curious. She'd tried to downplay it by being distant that morning, but she knew they were going to talk about this and she knew he had every right to ask. The question was: How did one explain living with a cheating, lying, thieving alcoholic to someone raised with such structure, such finery?

The minister of protocol turned out to be a short older woman whose green eyes lit when Ginny and Dominic entered the room.

She rose from her seat. "Prince Dominic!" She

rounded the desk and hugged him. "I hear congratulations are in order. You're about to have a baby!"

It was the first time anybody had actually been happy about her pregnancy or spoken of her baby as a baby, instead of a ruler or a prince or the guy who would be king. Ginny's heart filled with warmth and she forgot all about her dad, her past, her rubbish upbringing and the fear that someday she'd have to explain it all to Dominic.

The minister turned to Ginny. "And you." Her smile was warm, but didn't reach her eyes. "Congratulations on your upcoming wedding. Welcome to our home."

Stifling the urge to curtsy and the vague feeling that the minister didn't quite think her good enough, she said, "Thank you. But I still haven't made a decision on the marriage."

Dominic took over the introductions. "Virginia, this is Sally Peterson, our minister of protocol."

"You may call me Sally." She motioned to the chairs in front of her desk.

"Because Virginia is on the fence, I thought perhaps you could better explain to her why our getting married is a good idea."

"Okay." Sally folded her hands and set them on the desk. "What's the best way to explain this?" She thought for another second, then said, "Because your child will someday be our ruler, there isn't a court in the world that would refuse us the opportunity to train him, to bring him up to be our king. Which means you have four choices. First, marry Dom." She smiled at Dominic. "Second, don't marry Dom but live in the palace with your child to help raise him or her. Third, don't marry Dom, move back to the United States with a contingent of bodyguards and household servants until the child is twelve and will attend boarding school, and fourth, give up all rights."

Her voice softened. "I'm certain you don't want to give up all rights. Not marrying Dom, but living in the palace and helping raise your child makes sense, but will expose Dom to all kinds of gossip. He could be perceived as being unfit as a ruler if he couldn't even persuade the woman he'd gotten pregnant to marry him."

The thought of the ramifications for Dom made her blood run cold. She might not really know him, but she knew him enough that she could not let that happen to him. "What would happen if we got married?"

"You would need to be seen in public together at least twice before you would announce the quick wedding. We will also announce the pregnancy at the same time so that the rumors of a pregnancy don't take the sheen off your wedding day. The theory is if we get it out immediately it won't be 'news' anymore."

Exactly what Dom had told her.

He caught her gaze and smiled at her.

Once again she saw a glimpse of the guy who had whisked her away the night of their fateful dalliance. Stiff and formal or not, almost-complete stranger or not, he was the father of her child and his needs had to be considered.

"Plus, if you marry Dom, your position gives you a bit of power so to speak. You can use your celebrity to support causes. As someone who'd worked in education, you may wish to host events to raise awareness or to build schools anywhere in the world."

"Oh." That was amazing. Something she hadn't considered and something that would give her a chance to impact the *world*. Just the thought of it stole her breath. "That would be great."

"Plus," Sally said with a chuckle, "a royal wedding is fantastic. Your gown would be made by the designer of your choice." She laughed. "And money is no object. The guests will be royalty and dignitaries from every country in the world. You would get to meet your president."

"The president of the United States would be invited?"

"And he'd attend." Sally smiled. "Our royal family is influential. We don't just control waterways. We have oil, which gives us a seat in OPEC."

It was hard enough to adjust to the knowledge that Dominic was a royal. Now she was being told his small, seemingly insignificant country was powerful?

Oh, boy.

Dominic's hand stealthily slid from the arm of his chair over to her hand. He caught her pinkie with his, linking them.

She swallowed. He'd done that in the limo on the way to the club in Los Angeles. A small, sweet, simple gesture that made her heart catch and her breathing tremble. He recognized that all this information was becoming overwhelming for her. And the pinkie knot? It told her he was there for her.

Damn, but he could be sweet.

"But, as I mentioned, you have choices. And as I understand the situation, you and Dominic plan to divorce two years after the baby is born."

Dominic quietly said, "Yes."

The small, sweet gesture suddenly felt empty. Pointless. There was no need for them to be close. They just had to be friendly.

She pulled her hand away.

"In that case, most of your options still apply. Except

Dom wouldn't suffer the negative press of being unable to persuade you to marry him."

"I could return to the United States."

Sally laughed. "If, after years of being influential in education, of being someone known to the entire world, someone impacting the world, you still want to go back, then, yes."

Ginny smiled. Something about the way Sally kept highlighting the good part about staying in the country told her there was a catch, and she knew it had to have something to do with her child. "But the baby would go with me?"

Sally rose from the desk and walked to the front where she leaned against it. Her voice was soft, gentle. "Yes. As I'd said, that is an option. But it will require heightened security and teachers for home schooling unless you can find a private school that passes our tests. Then every time there was a ceremony, a formal dinner, a holiday, he'd have to be flown home." She shifted against the desk. "Ideally, our future ruler should be raised here. In the palace. It just makes things easier."

"Right."

Dominic faced her. "Our child needs to be acclimated into the life of a royal. Not rigidly, but to realize all monarchs and leaders are people, too. Countries are made up of people. Troubles are borne by people. Ruling is about people."

Caught in the gaze of his dark, dark eyes, she remembered why she'd fallen so hard for him the night she met him. He always knew the right thing to say.

Even if it was a modification of the truth.

Yesterday, he'd been smart enough to let her believe

returning home would be possible, when in reality it sounded as if it would be very hard on their child.

He hadn't out and out lied. In fact, if the option really was available for her to return to the United States, then he hadn't lied at all. But he was counting on her love for their baby to help her to see that returning home might be an option but it was a poor one.

She couldn't decide if he was manipulating her or trusting her, but after eighteen years of a bullying, manipulative father, that misstep made her stomach roil.

She rose. "You know what? I'm a bit tired. I think I should go back to the room."

He bounced to his feet. "Of course."

She faced Sally. "I'll need some help with etiquette. I know the basics but the specifics are way beyond what a high school guidance counselor needs to know. Even if I decide not to marry Dominic, I have an entire week here and I don't want to embarrass him."

Sally grabbed her calendar. "I'll make appointments for you."

"Just let me know when to be where."

Dominic laughed. "The teachers will come to our apartment. You're not just a guest of a prince. You're pregnant. We want to take care of you."

She ignored his laugh. Ignored the smile on his face. Ignored that he was solicitous about her pregnancy. Her dad had been exceptional at being sweet, being charming, when it suited him. She didn't want to think Dominic was like her dad, but the facts were out there plain and simple. He'd told her a half-truth the day before.

Still, she could deal with this. She was unfortunately good at dealing with people who told her half-truths.

She straightened her shoulders. "That's fine. I'm happy to have the sessions in your apartment."

She held her head high as she walked out of Sally's office, but her stomach churned.

Why was she even *considering* marrying a man who was a manipulator like her father?

CHAPTER THREE

DOMINIC HAD TO run to catch up to her. "What was that all about?"

"What?"

"Your sudden need to leave as if Sally had done something wrong."

"It wasn't Sally." She turned on him. "*You* led me to believe I could go home."

"The option is yours."

"Oh, sure, if I want to make our child's life a miserable succession of plane rides between Texas and Xaviera."

Not waiting for a reply, she raced to the elevator, punched the button and was inside before Dom had wrapped his head around what she'd said. He jumped into the plush car two seconds before the door would have closed.

"I'm sorry if the truth offends you."

She turned on him again, poking her index finger into his chest. "The truth? You told me half the truth, so I would get false hope. When the situation looked totally impossible, you held out the offer of being able to return home. Now that I'm adjusting to you, to your family and to people bowing to you, I'm told the option exists, but, oh, by the way, it will make your child's life suck."

He caught her finger. "What did you want me to say? No. You can't ever go home again?"

"Yes! I'm twenty-five years old. I handled two thousand kids for three years. I can handle this!"

The elevator door swished open. She yanked her finger from his hand and headed across the big square marble floor to the regal double doors of his apartment.

He ran after her, but didn't reach her until she was already in the sitting room of their apartment. When he did, he caught her arm and forced her to face him. "I will not have you be mad at me for something I didn't do! We didn't talk a lot yesterday. I gave you your bare-bones options because that's all you seemed to want to hear. Sally expanded on those options today. If you'd wanted the entire explanation yesterday, you should have stayed for it! Instead you said something about wanting to go to your room. I was fully prepared to talk it all out. *You* left."

He could see from the shifting expressions in her blue eyes that she knew what he said was true.

She dropped her head to her hands. "Oh, God. I'm sorry."

"It's okay."

She shook her head. "No. It isn't." She sucked in a breath. "Look, my dad was a hopeless alcoholic who was always lying to me. I have trust issues."

Glad to have his real Ginny back, Dom breathed a sigh of relief. "We all have trust issues."

He motioned for her to sit, so they could talk some more, but she shook her head. "I'm fine. Really. Tired, but fine."

A trained diplomat, he read the discretion in her answer and knew she didn't want to talk about this. Who would want to talk about a father who drank so much he'd clearly made her miserable? But at least he understood why she'd absurdly said she would have taken his family when she was a child.

"I probably also should have told you that all of this will be set out in an agreement."

"An agreement?"

"Yes, the legal office will draw up an agreement that sets out everything. Your responsibilities. Our responsibilities. What's required of you as mother to our future heir."

"You're going to put all this into an agreement?"

He chuckled. "You wouldn't?"

She considered that. "A written agreement would make things easier."

"It's one of the few documents that will remain totally secret. Because it's considered private, no one but you and I, the king and both of our counsels will even know it exists. But your jobs and responsibilities will be spelled out and so will mine. Plus, we can provide you with counsel who can assure you the agreement is fair. If you don't like who we provide, you can choose your own counsel."

She nodded.

"We're not trying to cheat you."

"Right."

"Really. And we don't sign the agreement until the day of the ceremony. So right up until the day we get married, you can change your mind."

"I'll just be doing it publicly."

He shrugged. "Sorry. The press sort of comes with the territory."

She didn't answer, but she'd definitely calmed down.

A written agreement seemed to suit her, but she still looked tired, worn. "Why don't you go lie down?"

She nodded and walked into her suite, closing the door behind her.

He gave her the morning to rest. When she came out at lunchtime, he pulled out her chair and she smiled.

Relieved that she really was okay, he said, "A simple coffee date has been arranged for us this afternoon."

"Then you'd better get someone up here to help me with wardrobe because I went through the clothes you had sent up yesterday and there isn't anything in there that I'd actually wear out in public."

"What about the white pants with the sweater?"

"Seriously? That blue sweater with the big anchor on the front? My mother would wear that."

"Okay. Fine. Right after lunch I'll have a clothier come up."

"Great." She looked at the food, then sat back as if discouraged.

"You don't like ham sandwiches?"

"They're great. I'm just not hungry."

He sucked in a breath. They'd had a misunderstanding but worked it out, and she'd taken a rest. When she'd come out of her suite, it was to eat lunch. Now suddenly she wasn't hungry?

"You had an orange for breakfast. You have to eat."

"Maybe I can get a cookie at the coffee shop."

He laughed, thinking she was joking. Seeing she wasn't, he frowned. "Seriously? That's going to be your food for the day? A cookie?"

"I told you. I'm not very hungry."

He supposed their situation would be enough to make a normal woman lose her appetite, but being married to him wasn't exactly the third circle of hell. Everything and anything she wanted could be at her disposal. There was no reason for her to refuse to eat.

"Okay. From here on out, you choose our menus."

She nodded. He felt marginally better. But what man in the world could possibly like the idea that just the thought of marrying him had taken away a woman's appetite?

Was she subtly saying he made her sick?

After a visit from the clothier, an hour's wait for clothing to be delivered and an hour for her to dress, they left the palace in his Mercedes. He drove, surprising her.

"We don't need a bodyguard?"

"They're discreetly behind us. This is supposed to look like a casual date."

"Ah."

He tried not to let her one-word answer grate against his skin, but it did. She wouldn't eat around him and her conversation had been reduced to one-word answers. He'd thought they'd resolved their issue, but maybe they hadn't? Or maybe the reality of marrying a prince was finally sinking in?

"You know you're going to have to say more than one word to me when we get into the coffee shop."

"Yes."

He gritted his teeth. "We could also use this time to chitchat so that when we get out of the car, we'll already be engaged in conversation the way normal people would be."

"I know all about being a normal person." She flicked her gaze to him. "You, on the other hand, are wearing a white shirt out for coffee."

"I'm a prince."

"You're also a person, supposedly out with a woman he likes. A woman he's comfortable with. White shirt does not say *comfortable*."

"Oh, and scruffy jeans does?"

She laughed. "Are you kidding? Scruffy jeans is the very definition of *comfortable*."

"You look like you're going to the trash yard."

"I look like an American girl on a date with a prince she just met. I am playing the part. As our dates get more serious so will my wardrobe."

Unexpectedly seeing her reasoning, he sighed. "Okay. I get it. Just don't make fun of the white shirt."

"Fine."

He glanced in the rearview mirror and saw not just the Mercedes with his bodyguards, but also the usual assortment of paparazzi. Satisfied, he finished the drive to the ocean-side coffee shop.

Xaviera's warm sun beat down on him as he walked around to the passenger's side and opened the door for Ginny. He took her hand and helped her out, to the whir of cameras. She stepped out, one blue-jeans-clad leg at a time, wedge sandals, short blue T-shirt and big sunglasses, all looking very normal to him in the parking lot of a beach café.

She really had been right about her very casual clothes.

Standing in front of him, she caught his gaze and smiled, and his heart—which had been thundering in his chest from fear of the first step of their charade—slowed down. He hadn't forgotten how beautiful she was, but somehow or another the sunlight seemed to bring out the best in her rich yellow hair and tanned skin. She might not be royalty or someone accustomed to the public eye, like an actress or model, but she was every bit as beautiful—if not more beautiful because she was genuine.

The cameras whirred again.

She whispered, "What do we do? Do we wave?"

"We ignore them."

She peeked up at him. "Really?"

He laughed, took her hand and led her to the café door. "Yes. We know they are there. But we also know they are always there, even if, for us, they have no purpose. Unlike an actor or actress, we don't need them to enhance our visibility. We tolerate them. Thus, we ignore them."

"Got it."

He held the door open for her. The press rushed up behind them, but his bodyguards closed the door on them. Two things happened simultaneously. The press opened the door and crammed in behind the bodyguards, their cameras whirring. And Marco, café owner, greeted them.

"Prince Dominic!" He bowed. "It's an honor."

"Can I have my usual, Marco? And—" Oh, dear God. First complication. He could not order coffee for a pregnant woman. He faced Ginny. "What would you like, Ginny?"

As soon as he said her name, the reporters began shouting, "Ginny! Ginny! Look here, Ginny!"

She slid off her sunglasses. Doing as he'd told her, she ignored the press. "How about some water? It's hot."

The press laughed. "Did you not know our weather was hot?"

"Where are you from?"

"How old are you?"

"How did you meet?"

"How long have you been dating?"

Dominic also ignored them. "Just water? What about that cookie?"

Marco said, "I have a cookie that will make you happy to be alive."

Ginny laughed. "That'd be great."

"You sound American."

He saw Ginny waver. The questions directed at her were hard for her to ignore. And the press began closing in on them. Even with his two bodyguards standing six inches away, the reporters and photographers bent around them, shouted questions and took pictures as Marco made Dom's coffee, retrieved a bottle of water and wrapped a cookie in a napkin.

Dom took their items and turned to say, "Let's go out to the deck by the dock," but, as he turned, he saw her sway. Before he could blink, she began to crumble.

He dropped his coffee, the water and the cookie to the counter and just barely caught her before she hit the floor.

The cameras whirred. A gasp went up from the crowd. Dominic's bodyguards turned to help him as Marco came out from behind the counter, broom in hand.

"Get out of here!" He waved the broom at the paparazzi. "Get out, you brood of vipers!" He glanced behind the counter. "Antonella. I chase them out. You lock the door!"

Down on one knee, holding Ginny, Dominic cast Marco a grateful look as the coffeehouse owner and Dom's bodyguards shooed the press out of his shop and Antonella locked the door behind them.

Ginny's eyes slowly blinked open. "It's so hot."

He sort of smiled. She was so fragile and so beautiful, and holding her again took him back to their night of dancing in LA and making love in her condo. A million feelings trembled through him. Brilliant memories. A sense of peace that had intermixed with their fun. The wonderful, almost-overwhelming sensation of being able to be himself because she was so comfortable being herself.

"You're adding to the heat by wearing jeans."

"Trying to look normal."

Her skin was clammy. Her eyes listless and dull. His happy, beautiful one-night stand memories dropped like a rock, as his heart squeezed with fear. "We need to get you to the hospital."

"You're sending a pregnant woman to the hospital for fainting? You haven't been around pregnant women much have you?"

"That's all this is?"

She drew in a breath and suddenly looked stronger. "Heat. Pregnancy. Nerves. Take your pick."

He said, "Right." Then nodded at Marco. "Open her water."

The solicitous shop owner did as he was told. He handed the opened bottle to Dominic, who held it out to her. She took a few sips.

Dominic sighed, grateful she was coming back but so scared internally that he shook from it. His heart had about leaped out of his chest when he saw her falling. "You should probably have a bite or two of the cookie. I told you to eat lunch."

She smiled. "Wasn't hungry."

Antonella brought over the cookie. "You eat."

Ginny sat up a bit and took the cookie from Antonella's hands.

"Maybe we should get you to a chair?"

She laughed. "I feel safer down here. No cameras. No one can see me through the windows."

He felt it, too. Behind the tables and chairs between them and the doorway, he felt totally protected from the press.

She ate a few bites of her cookie, drank the entire bottle of water and held out her hand to him. "We can stand now."

"We're going to have to go back to the car though a crowd of reporters and photographers who just saw you faint. If you thought their questions were bad before this—" he caught her gaze "—now they are going to be horrific. A tidal wave of jumbled words and noisy cameras. Are you up for this?"

"I'm fine."

"Right. As soon as we get home, I'm having you checked out by the doctor."

"I would expect nothing less from a man accustomed to bossing people around."

His fear for her wouldn't recede and she didn't seem to be taking any of this seriously. "Stop joking. You fainted."

"On a hot day, after not eating." She smiled suddenly, pushed herself to her tiptoes and kissed his cheek. "I'm fine."

The unexpected kiss went through him like a warm spring breeze. He told himself not to make too much of it, but how could he not when color was returning to her cheeks and she was smiling, really smiling, for the first time since their argument that morning.

Wanting to get her home, Dominic said, "Let's go."

But before they could walk to the door, Marco hugged her and then Antonella hugged her. Dominic finally noticed the few stragglers sitting at the café tables, necks craned to see what was going on. One or two whispered, but in general, they'd given them privacy.

Leading her to the door, he addressed them, "Thank you all for your consideration."

People nodded and smiled and a few said, "You're welcome." Then they reached the door. The lock clicked as Antonella sprang it.

He said, "Ready?"

Ginny nodded.

He opened the door to the whir of cameras and shouts of questions. "How are you?"

"Why did you faint?"

"What's your last name?"

"Are you pregnant?"

Dominic's steps faltered.

But Ginny slid her sunglasses on her face and smiled at them. "I didn't eat lunch." She turned to Dominic and entwined her arm with his. "Dom told me to eat lunch but—" She held out a leg. "Look at these jeans. They are to die for and I wanted them to fit." She smiled again. "American girls, right? We love our jeans and we want them to look perfect."

Then she turned them in the direction of his Mercedes. His bodyguards created a path for them to walk.

He opened the door for her.

She slid inside. Before Dom could close the door, she gave a final wave to the press. "I'm fine," she called out to them. "And, I swear, I will eat before we come out again."

Walking around the hood of his car, he heard the rumble of laughter. He peeked up to see the smiles of approval on the faces of those in the crowd. And why not? She was beautiful, approachable, *likable*.

But he also saw a few reporters frowning in his direction. He saw the ones on their cell phones talking feverishly.

He slid into the car. "You know your pregnancy's out now, right?"

"Yup." She caught his gaze. "Looks like we won't need a second date."

"You're saying yes?"

She nodded.

He took her hand and lifted it to his lips. "Thank you."

"Oh, don't thank me. I have a feeling we're in for one hell of a ride."

CHAPTER FOUR

THEY SCHEDULED A press conference for nine o'clock the next morning in the press room of the palace. The king announced his son's marriage to Virginia Jones of Texas in the United States, a former guidance counselor. Then he gave the podium to Dominic.

As Ginny expected, the resounding cry that rose from the crowd was… "Is Ginny pregnant?"

Another man might have been cowed, embarrassed or even unprepared. Ginny knew Dom had rehearsed every possible scenario of this moment into the wee hours of the morning with someone from his staff.

So she wasn't surprised when he smiled and said, "Yes."

The swish and whir of cameras filled the room. Several people called, "Ginny, look here."

But she kept her eyes trained on Dominic because that's what *her* two hours of training the night before had been about. That and choosing something to wear. After a doctor had seen her and pronounced her well, a clothier had arrived with swatches and catalogs. Sally from the protocol office had wanted her in a raspberry-colored suit. The king had thought she'd look more dignified in a white suit. But she'd reminded them that she'd fainted because she was *pregnant* and had gotten too hot. Her choice for the press conference had been a simple green dress with thin straps and a pale green cardigan—which she could remove, she reminded the king—if she got too hot.

The king had scowled, but Dominic had suddenly said, "I think she's right."

All eyes had turned to him. He'd shrugged. "You're not the ones who had to watch her fall. I barely caught her. I don't think we want to risk having that happen again."

Nope. If there was one thing Ginny knew, it was that she did not want to faint again. Seeing ten pictures of herself crumpling to a coffee-shop floor in the newspapers that morning had been enough to cure her of ever wanting to faint in public again.

But Dominic standing up for her choice had caused her breath to quietly catch. Her simple pregnancy might impact an entire kingdom—and maybe someday even the world—but this was her *baby*. And Dom's.

When he stood up for her, he caught her gaze, and in that second a wave of feeling had almost made her dizzy. They'd created a child and were getting married—temporarily. He'd warned her not to spin fantasies of permanency with him, and she wasn't, but with a baby on the way and so many people telling them what to do, she didn't see how they could get through the next few months without forming a team.

Which made it a terrible, terrible thing that she'd compared him to her father. Because no matter how hard she tried, she couldn't stop doing it. Not because she genuinely believed Dom was like her dad, but because she was so afraid. Living with her dad had been a nightmare. Only a fool would deliberately enter that kind of situation again.

So he couldn't be like her dad. He *couldn't*. Yet something about this situation, and Dom, set off warning signals that would not let her relax.

Watching Dominic speak now, she waited for his signal for her to join him at the podium. He fielded a question or two about how they met, then, just as they'd practiced, he turned to her with a smile and said, "Why don't we have Ginny join us to help answer some questions?"

In her high-heeled white sandals that perfectly offset the pretty green dress, she carefully walked to the podium. He slid his arm around her waist, bringing her closer to the microphones. Questions filled the air.

"Have you found a dress?"

"Are you having morning sickness?"

She heard the questions, but looking up at Dominic, all she saw were those onyx eyes filled with expectation. Could she stand up for him? Would she stand up for him? Would she protect his reputation as the future king the way he'd stood up for her the night before? Was she willing to fully commit to the charade?

Just as she couldn't quite get herself to trust him, the question in his eyes told her he didn't entirely trust her, either.

Which made them even.

If there was one thing she'd learned about partnerships, it was that they ran best when the partners really were even. Oddly, this deal would work not because they trusted each other, but because they didn't.

"Are you a real live Cinderella?"

That question made her laugh and brought her out of her reverie. She faced the sea of press crowded into the small room.

"Yes. I do feel like Cinderella. No, I haven't even

chosen a designer to make my dress. So I'll need all four weeks before the wedding just to find something to wear." When the reporters laughed, she smiled. "And no morning sickness."

She paused long enough to give Dominic her best fake loving smile, deferring to him, the way she'd been taught to the night before. When their gazes met, she could see he was pleased with how she handled herself. She recognized that his happy expression was part of their act, but he'd looked at her exactly that way the night they'd gone clubbing. The night they'd created their baby.

Her heart kicked against her ribs. A flash of memories flooded her brain. Kissing in the limo. Laughing at stupid things. Not a care in the world. And for one foolish second, she wished they could be those two people again. Two people just having fun. Not making a commitment—

She quickly looked away. Things like that, staring into his fathomless eyes, longing for a chance just to enjoy each other, would get her into trouble.

She faced the reporters. "So I won't faint again." She winced. "That is if I listen to Dom and actually eat breakfast and lunch."

A quiet chuckle went up from the group as they scribbled in notebooks.

The questions started again.

"What about your job?"

"Will you miss working?"

"What was it like growing up with an alcoholic dad?"

"Did you spin daydreams as a little girl that you'd someday marry a prince?"

The room suddenly got hot. She hadn't expected her

dad's life to escape scrutiny. She simply hadn't expected it to come up so soon.

She pushed her hair off her face, buying time, hoping to cool her forehead a bit before sweat began to bead on it. "I love my job." She answered the first and second questions together since they were easy, as she dreadfully scrambled in her head to think of how to answer the third. "If it were possible to be a princess *and* be a guidance counselor, I'd do both. As it is, my duty lies with Xaviera and our baby." She laughed. "My mom reminded me that even if my baby wasn't a future king, he'd still take up all my time and shift my priorities."

Before she could deal with question three, two other reporters raised their hands and called out, "So you've spoken to your mom and have her blessing?" and "Where is your mom?"

"My mom is finishing out her semester," she said, then suddenly wished her mom didn't have to work. Being alone in a strange country, in a white-hot spotlight with a guy she'd liked a lot was making her crazy. She had to remember he wasn't fun-loving Dom. He was Prince Dominic. And this marriage wasn't real. Hell, this whole situation was barely real.

"She has a few more weeks of school, but she'll be here for the wedding."

"I'm still waiting for an answer about your childhood with an alcoholic father."

The sweat arrived, beading on her forehead. A hot, dizzying wave passed through her, weakening her knees, just as it had two seconds before she'd fainted the day before.

"My father was sick," she said quietly, praying her legs would continue to hold her. "He also died when I was eighteen. I barely remember that part of my life."

That wasn't really a lie, more of an exaggeration. She didn't want to remember, so she spent her days refusing to even think about those years.

"As for whether or not I spun fantasies about marrying a prince." She smiled. "I hadn't. I was a very pragmatic child, enamored with my mom's love of her classes and students. But I'm glad I met Dominic."

Again, not a lie. She *was* glad she had met him. She'd loved their night out. It was being in cahoots with him, putting so much of her life into another person's hands, that caused fear to course through her. Especially after the mention of her dad. After being reminded that trusting the wrong person could suck the life out of your soul, reduce you to someone who suspiciously weighed every word and soon didn't trust anyone. Someone who protected herself by staying in her room, alone and lonely.

She did not want that to be her life again.

This time when she turned to smile at Dominic, she knew her eyes were dull and listless.

She wasn't surprised when he said, "And that's all for this morning. Our press office has issued a release with all relevant information."

He led her off the podium and then out of the room, behind the king, who turned to her with a satisfied look. "You lasted much longer than I predicted."

She winced. "Thank you, I think."

"Well, it's a compliment to an extent. I'm still not sure I trust your fashion sense. And I'm not at all pleased that you didn't warn us about your dad."

Her stomach churned. She'd buried her dad seven years ago, but here she was hiding him again, protecting him again— "I…"

Dominic stepped up. "I knew about her dad. My

security detail investigated everything." He caught Ginny's gaze. "I admit we glossed over his alcoholism because he's been dead for seven years. But no one kept it a secret."

She swallowed. Every time she looked in his eyes, she had no question about why he'd so easily been able to seduce her. But every time he talked he reminded her that she didn't belong here in his life, and how difficult the next years would be. "I guess you did that while we were waiting for the paternity results."

"Actually, we investigated you when we were told you would be my liaison at the school." He faced the king. "And you have a full report on Ginny's life in your office. Her father is in there."

King Ronaldo said, "I don't know how I missed it."

"You missed it because he's barely a footnote. He was never arrested. Never in the papers. Never anything. And now he's gone. Ginny and I talked about this a bit yesterday and the end result was I decided there's no real reason to put her through the memories by insisting she give us details."

He smiled slightly at her.

She tried to smile back. But an odd feeling tumbled through her. Not quite a nudge that she should trust him, the feeling told her at the very least she should appreciate the way he'd saved her from having to relive a part of her life that was gone. Past. She shouldn't have to explain it.

Sally said, "Yes, well, Prince Dominic, you should have bought this to your father's attention instead of expecting him to find it in a report."

Dom faced Sally, who stood with her arms crossed, clearly unhappy with him. He said, "I'll remember next time," but when he turned to Ginny he winked.

The weird feeling tumbled through her again.

Sally lifted her clipboard. "Okay, Ms. Jones, you have a few people coming to the apartment for lessons today. Mostly protocols and etiquettes. At four, the clothier and I will be bringing catalogs of various designers' work so you can begin the process of screening designers for your dress." She flipped a page. "Dom, I believe you're due in parliament this afternoon."

Dominic caught Ginny's hand. "Then I guess we better get back to the apartment and arrange for lunch."

Sally said, "Fine—"

But Dominic didn't wait for the rest of her answer. He turned and walked away, leading Ginny down several halls. He walked so fast, she had to skip to keep up with him in her high, high heels, but the air that whooshed past them was cool, and she suddenly felt like laughing. Not only had they survived the press, but Dominic had taken her side—again.

When the elevator door closed behind them, Ginny said, "That was awesome."

"What? You liked being interviewed by reporters?"

She batted a hand. "I could take that or leave that. What I loved was you walking away from Sally."

Dom spared her a glance, then he grinned. "She's protocol office so she basically runs everything. It's fun every once in a while to remind her that she works for me."

"Oh, so you're a tough guy now?"

He laughed. "I told you being a king is all about being respected."

"Well, in that case, let me say you got some votes of confidence from me."

He turned. "Really?"

"Yes. Last night when you said we should use my

dress choice and this morning when you let me answer my own questions from the press—those were good. But not letting Sally push me around? Or your dad? Those were better. I… Well, I felt like a real person."

"You are a real person."

She laughed, but something inside nudged her to talk, to at least trust him enough to tell him the basics. "I know that. But my upbringing was awful. There are more chances that I'm going to embarrass you than make you proud."

"Are you kidding? Your first public act was to faint, then pretend it was no big deal when you walked back into the fray of reporters to get to the car. You waved and told them you were fine as if they were a bunch of friends hanging out on a street corner." He laughed. "I think they don't know what to do with you."

"So confusion is the way to go, if I can't beguile them with my good looks and charm?"

He sneaked another peek at her as the elevator door opened on the big square foyer before his apartment. "Oh, I wouldn't discount your charm just yet."

She looked up at him. He gazed down at her. With the huge hall just outside the door empty and quiet, the tiny elevator suddenly felt intimate.

Gazing into his eyes, she remembered how he'd pulled her to him outside her apartment door and kissed her like a man so crazy about a woman he couldn't resist her.

So maybe he did think she had charm.

The elevator door began to close and without looking away Dominic caught it, forcing it open again.

"We better go."

"Yeah."

Neither of them moved. Something hummed between

them. She'd say it was the same something that had brought him to her condo door all those weeks ago, the same something that drew them to her bed, except in the past two days she'd made him laugh and he wasn't going to make her talk about her dad.

He took a step closer to her and her breath shivered. Her lips tingled from wanting to kiss him. But he stayed where he was, close enough to touch, but not making a move to kiss her, though his eyes shimmered with need.

The air filled with something hot and tempting. She knew she could easily label this lust, but she knew something else was at work here. They really were forming a team. And the pull of that, the longing not to be alone in this deal, fighting for herself and her rights, but having somebody fight with her, was even stronger than the lust that had driven them that night.

That scared her silly.

But his gaze held hers.

And everything inside her trembled with yearning.

She longed for the day she'd met him, when she didn't fear their future because she didn't think they had a future, and she wondered what it would be like to let her guard down again—

But Dom had warned her not to spin fairy tales. And life had taught her that good things could turn bad in the blink of an eye. Not more than twenty minutes ago, she'd been worried about comparing him to her dad. Now she wanted to kiss him? To trust him?

Everything was happening too fast.

This was a ruse. Nothing more. And she was going to get hurt if she didn't stop trying to spin that fairy tale.

She turned and walked out of the elevator to the apartment and to her suite.

CHAPTER FIVE

DOMINIC ATE A very quiet, disappointing lunch. No matter how he tried to engage Ginny, she'd smile distantly and pop a bite of food into her mouth so she didn't have to talk to him. Glad to see her eating for the sake of the baby, he couldn't allow himself the luxury of being upset that she wasn't talking to him.

Still, it made him nuts.

They were perfectly fine in that elevator until the conversation about her charming the press. She *could* charm the press. And without effort. But something about that one simple comment had made her quiet. Distant.

He probably shouldn't have mentioned it. Her ability with them was so natural that if he hadn't pointed it out to her, she would have used it without thought. But he liked talking to her and he liked it when they were getting along. Their natural connection would be what would make the charade work.

Then they'd had that moment of looking into each other's eyes, and for twenty seconds he'd thought he wouldn't be able to resist kissing her. But he *had*. He'd remembered his dad, the weakness that plagued him after Dom's mother's death. He knew he couldn't afford a marriage with real emotion. And when he kissed her, he felt things he couldn't define or describe. So he stepped back, away from a kiss he wanted, to prove he didn't *need* it.

That should have made her happy. God knew it made him happy to see he could resist her. She should be happy, too. Instead, she was distant.

He left her after lunch and spent four grueling hours in parliament. Tired and somewhat disgusted, he returned to his palace apartment to find Sally and Joshua, the clothier, sitting on one sofa with Ginny alone on the sofa across from them. Though Sally was frustrated, Joshua looked to be the picture of patience as he ran down the benefits of a list of designers.

Ginny frowned. "I know what I like. I know what I look good in. It just seems so sterile to be picking a gown this way. I always imagined myself trying things on."

Joshua smiled patiently. "Most women would kill for the chance to choose a designer to make a unique gown."

Ginny only sighed and glanced at the photo array of designers and their creations.

Sally shook her head. "What difference does it make? For Pete's sake. This wedding is just for show. It's not real. The gown doesn't have to reflect *you*. It just has to be beautiful. Something fit for a princess."

Ginny finally noticed Dom standing in the foyer by the door, but she quickly looked away. Still, he'd seen the naked misery in her eyes.

She straightened her shoulders, as if seeing him reminded her of her duty to him, and she pointed at one of the photo arrays. "This one. I'd like this designer."

Sally sighed with relief and rose. "We'll contact him."

Joshua rose, too. He bowed. "I am at your service."

Sally said, "Good because she still has a wardrobe to choose. Two pair of jeans and a green dress with cardigan won't be enough clothes for two days let alone over two years."

Joshua on her heels, Sally headed for the white double doors. "You'll be required to meet with Joshua again tomorrow afternoon, Ginny."

"That's Ms. Jones," Dominic said, suddenly annoyed. "She may not be a princess yet. But she will be. And when she is she will be your boss."

Sally quietly gasped and stepped back, but she quickly recovered. Bowing to Dominic, she said, "Yes, Your Majesty."

Joshua all but quivered with fear. New to the palace, because the king and the two princes rarely required help in choosing suits or having them made, he glanced from Dom to Sally, wide-eyed.

Sally opened the door and left. Joshua scampered after her.

Ginny blew her breath out on a long sigh. "You shouldn't have yelled at her. It wasn't her fault that I'm having trouble choosing. And our time is running out. She's right to be annoyed with me."

He walked to the bar and poured himself a Scotch. "Oh, sweetie. You have so much to learn about being a princess."

"I'm not going to be vapid and spoiled."

"Of course, you're not. But you can't let staff belittle you."

"As I said, she was right to be annoyed with me."

"Again. No. You are the member of the royal family here. If you want to take until the day before the wedding to choose your dress, that's what you do. Then *they* scramble."

She laughed.

He sat beside her on the sofa. "So, are you really happy with the designer you chose?"

She shrugged. "He's as good as any."

He caught her chin and nudged her to face him. "As good as any isn't good enough. I want you to be happy the day you get married. It may not be forever, but it's your first wedding."

"That's what I keep thinking."

"So what would you do if you were getting married for keeps?"

"I'd have a lot of pink roses."

"What else?"

"My two friends would be bridesmaids."

"You can have that." He sipped his Scotch. "What else?"

"I don't know. I always imagined my mom and me picking things out." She peeked up at him. "She has great taste."

He laughed. "Really?"

"Well, actually, we have about the same taste. But picking a gown is just something a girl wants to do with her mom. You know. Second opinion and all that." She took a deep breath, blew it out, then looked Dom in the eye. "My picture is going to go around the world. I'd like for it to be a good one."

He nodded. "That's something I'm so accustomed to I forget that others aren't." He rose from the sofa. "I have a dinner meeting tonight that's going to segue into a bigger meeting with several members of parliament. Why don't you call your friends on Skype and invite them to be your bridesmaids?"

She looked up at him, her eyes round and blue and honest. She was one of the most naturally beautiful women he'd ever met. She was also being a much better sport about this marriage than a lot of women would be. She hadn't asked for anything. She just did as she was told. And if she didn't talk to him, maybe that was his fault? He'd told her not to expect a long, happy marriage. If she held herself back, maybe that's what she felt she needed to do.

"Really? I can have bridesmaids?"

"As many as you want." On impulse he bent down and kissed her cheek. "Would a wedding without bridesmaids really look authentic?"

She shook her head.

"So call them."

Ginny watched Dom leave the sitting room and head for his bedroom suite, fighting that feeling again. Except this time, she named it. She wasn't worried about liking him or even being attracted to him. What she was feeling—or maybe recognizing—was that he was a nice guy. A good person. She thanked God he'd reminded her that the wedding needed to "look" authentic to serve his purpose. Otherwise, she might have melted right there at his feet.

She could resist the solemn guy, the one who would be king someday, who wanted everything to be perfect. The other guy, the sweet one who tried to make her happy? That was the guy who had been staring at her in the elevator. The one she'd wanted to kiss. He was the one she had to watch out for.

She returned to her room, found her laptop and connected with her two best friends on Skype. They knew she was pregnant, of course. She'd gone to them for guidance. She'd also called them the day she'd fainted, when she'd agreed to marry Dom. They were not surprised to be receiving invitations to be bridesmaids.

That little piece of normalcy lifted her spirits. It wasn't going to be a real marriage but it was going to be a real wedding, and she was going to look pretty and have her friends with her. They would keep her occupied the week before the big day. And, in a good mood, she'd be better able to look happy for the ceremony.

The next morning at breakfast, she showed her appreciation to Dominic by asking him how his meetings had gone the night before.

He winced. "There are one or two people who fear we are making an alliance with the United States by bringing you into the royal family."

She laughed. When he didn't, she said, "Really? Seriously? They think marrying a commoner from the United States is a lead-in to a treaty?"

"My brother will be marrying a woman as part of a treaty. Why would you be surprised our government is questioning my marriage?"

She shook her head and went back to her oatmeal. "I forget that your country looks at marriage differently."

"It's not really my country that looks at marriage differently. It's the royal family and what's expected of us. I'll be spending weeks alleviating the fears of several members of parliament, assuring them that our marriage is not part of a big master plan."

Taking a bite of oatmeal, she nodded. "I get it. It's something you shouldn't think you have to do, but you will. Just like I'll be spending two hours with Sally's staff today, learning how to curtsy."

"I thought curtsying was out. Old school. Something nobody did anymore."

"According to Sally's morning memo, there are some

small eastern European countries that still believe in it. I just hope we don't run into any of those royal families when I'm big-as-a-house pregnant. I can't imagine curtsying and balancing twenty-five pounds of stomach."

He laughed. "You're going to make an interesting princess."

"Lucky for you, it's only for a little over two years."

He said, "Uh-huh," and went back to reading his newspaper.

Ginny didn't care. Their conversation proved that she could talk to the "nice" Dominic and not get carried away. They did not have to be best friends. But they did have to get along. They had to look good together in public. They needed to know enough about each other that their charade appeared to be real. And this morning it was clear they were succeeding.

If there was a little rumble in her heart about wasting her wedding, a beautiful wedding, on a fake marriage, she silenced it. She'd never imagined herself getting married. Living with her dad had scared her off that. She'd never allow herself to let her guard down with a man enough to get serious enough to get married. So this was her wedding. Her one shot at being a bride. She'd be a fool not to make it as perfect as she could.

At four o'clock that afternoon, Dom unexpectedly returned to the apartment. As they had the day before, Joshua and Sally sat on the sofa across from her. The photo arrays and designer lists were with them.

She faced the door with a smile. "I thought you had more glad-handing to do."

He walked in and said, "I do. But I was the one who told Sally and Joshua to bring the designer lists up to you again. I wanted to make sure we were all on the same page."

"They told me you said I wasn't sure about the designer." She bit her lip, not happy that something she'd told him had become an issue.

He caught her gaze. "I want you to be sure."

The feeling whooshed through her again. The one that told her he was looking out for her because he was a nice guy. He might not love her. He might not even know her well enough to like her. But he was a nice enough guy that he wanted her to be happy.

"Okay."

Even as she said that, the big double doors of Dominic's apartment opened. "Ginny?"

Ginny's head snapped up. "Mom?"

She blinked as she saw her tall, slim mother race into the sitting room from the echoing foyer. Wearing a tan pantsuit that the king probably would have loved for its dignity, she ran over to Ginny.

Ginny rose and was enfolded into her mom's hug. After a long squeeze, she said, "Let me look at you!"

"Why aren't you in school?"

"Dom called. He said you needed help with your gown."

Her throat closed and tears welled in her eyes. This act of Dominic's was a little more difficult to call the actions of a nice guy trying to keep her happy. Having her mother flown to Xaviera was so kind it made her chest tight.

"I don't exactly need help. I just love your opinions."

Her mom said, "Even better." Then she faced Joshua and Sally, both of whom had risen. "And you must be Sally and Joshua."

Sally bowed slightly. Joshua said, "She's actually very clear about what she wants. I think she just needs your reassurance."

"Joshua, Sally, this is my mother, Rose Jones."

Ginny's mom smiled broadly. Her pretty blond hair had a hint of pink in it, because—well, she was a Texas girl, who'd grown up dancing to the Beach Boys and riding horses, and that crazy part of her had no intention of dying. "Let me see the designers and the dresses."

Joshua immediately handed over the photo array panels, but Ginny stepped away and slid around to the back of the couch where Dom stood.

He raised his eyebrows in question. "What?"

"You told my mom I needed help?"

He shook his head. "No, I called her and said I wanted you to be happy planning this wedding."

The sweetness of the gesture filled her heart. "I would have been okay."

"And the wedding would have looked fake."

This time the reminder that he didn't want the wedding to look fake didn't go through her like a knife. It was their deal. He'd always been up-front about their deal.

The crazy feeling she got around nice Dom morphed into something soft and happy. "We're going to have a beautiful wedding."

He smiled. "Yes, we are."

The air between them changed. For a few seconds, she debated springing to her tiptoes and hugging him, but that wasn't really acceptable, either.

Holding his gaze, she took a step back, then another, suddenly realizing why she kept getting odd nudges. After decades of surface relationships that she'd ended before she even knew the guy she was involved with, she'd managed to never really know anyone, never get beyond platitudes. But planning a fake wedding? Living in the same apartment with Dom? Coconspirators to protect their child? She was getting to know him. And she liked him. A lot more than she'd ever liked any man.

And he'd warned her not to spin a fairy-tale fantasy because he didn't want a marriage with emotion.

CHAPTER SIX

TWO DAYS LATER, Dom strode down the marble-floored hall to the double doors of his apartment. Since Rose had arrived, his home had become like a beehive. Where Ginny might be shy about creating a wardrobe, Rose had taken to the task as if she was born to it. Designers had been called in. Dresses and pants arrived for fittings. Two styles of wedding dresses had been chosen and Alfredo Larenzo, an Italian designer, had been hired to create them.

With a wince, he partially opened one of the two double doors, sticking his head in far enough to see into the living room. Which was, mercifully, empty. For a second, he hoped that Ginny and her mom had gone out for lunch, but his chest pinched. Since Rose had arrived, he'd also barely seen Ginny.

Not that he missed her. He didn't really know her. They were in a fake situation. There was nothing to miss. The thing was, he liked seeing her. Usually, she was funny. After four-hour sessions in parliament, funny was welcome. So he didn't miss her. He missed her silliness.

Comfortable with that assessment, he walked past the double sofas, over to the bar. When he turned to pour his Scotch, he saw the door to Ginny's suite door was open. And there she stood, in little pink panties and a pink lace bra. A short man wearing spectacles and a white shirt with the sleeves rolled to his elbows had a tape measure around her hips. Her mom stood with her back to the door, obviously supervising.

Dom stared. He'd forgotten how perfect she was. With full breasts, a sweet dip for a waist and hips that flared just enough for a man to run his hand along, she had what most men would consider a perfect figure.

The short, dark-haired guy raised the tape measure to her waist and Dom followed every movement of the man's hands, remembering the smoothness of her shape, the silkiness of her skin. The tailor whipped the tape around and snapped the two ends together in the middle, right above her belly button and Dominic's head tilted.

Right there…

Right below that perfect belly button…

Was his child.

His child.

His hand went limp and the glass he was holding fell to the bar with a thump.

Ginny's head snapped up and she turned to see him standing there, staring. Their eyes met. And it hit him for the very first time, not that she was pregnant, but that the baby she carried was *his*.

His baby.

He'd created a life.

Rose turned, saw him and walked to the door. "Sorry, Dom. Didn't realize you were home."

And she closed the door.

Dominic stared at it. The whole thing about the baby didn't floor him as much as the realization that the baby was in Ginny's stomach. In a few weeks that flat tummy of hers would be round. She'd gain weight. Be miserable. Probably grouchy. Her feet would swell. She'd be clumsy—in front of millions. And then she'd spend God knew how long in labor.

Because of his baby.

Ginny's suite door opened and she walked out, tying the belt of a pink satin robe around her.

"Was there something you wanted?"

He stared at her, his chest tight, his mind numb. Up until that very moment he hadn't really considered how much Ginny was doing for him. Oh, he understood the loss of her job, but he suddenly saw the other things— losing her friends, living away from her mom, stretching her tummy to unknown limits, changing everything.

For his baby.

"Dom?"

He shook his head to clear it. "Sorry. I'm taking a break and thought I'd come up and see if you're ready for the formal dinner tonight with the ambassador."

She angled her thumb behind her, pointing at her suite door. "That's what the little guy with the moustache is doing. Final fitting for a dress Sally tells me your dad is going to have a fit over."

A laugh bubbled up, but he squelched it. "You can't always push my dad's buttons."

She shrugged. "I'm bored."

His laughter died. "Really?"

"No! Absolutely not. I'm getting fitted for a billion dresses and three-point-five-million pair of jeans. I never realized how many clothes a princess was expected to have."

"So you're not bored?"

"No. I just have a style." She shrugged and the pretty, shiny pink robe shifted over her sun-kissed shoulders.

He remembered biting those shoulders, nibbling her

neck, rubbing his entire body over the length of her entire body.

"And, I swear, I'm not going overboard with sexy clothes. I'm just not going to dress like a grandma."

He cleared his throat. "I get it about not wanting to dress like a grandma. But be careful."

"You don't think it's time for someone to bring your dad into the twenty-first century?"

"If you can bring him in without the press having a field day, then give it your best shot."

She smiled, turned and walked back to her room. He watched every swish of the satin over her round bottom.

"Dinner's at eight, right?"

She called the question over her shoulder, her shiny yellow hair flowing to the middle of her back, accenting that curved waist that led to her perfect butt.

Dominic licked his suddenly dry lips. "Yes, eight. But we need to be in my dad's quarters at seven so that we all arrive in the dining room together, long before the ambassador so we can greet him."

"Piece of cake."

She opened the door to her suite and walked inside, leaving him alone in the living room again.

He tugged his tie away from his throat. A year of celibacy with her was not going to be easy.

He threw back the shot of Scotch and returned to his office for a few hours of admin work. When he entered the apartment again, Ginny's door was closed. He suspected she was getting ready for the dinner, so he went to his quarters, showered and put on the trousers and white shirt of his tux.

He managed the bow tie the way he could since he was eight, but the onyx-and-diamond cuff links, heirlooms with tricky catches, wouldn't lock.

He looked at his door and smiled. For the first time in his life he had a woman. In his quarters. About to marry him. Why shouldn't he take advantage?

Walking past the white sofas in the sitting room, he reminded himself that another man engaged to a gorgeous woman would find much better ways to take advantage of the situation, but he sought only help with cuff links. He was insane.

He knocked on her door.

"Yes."

"It's me, Dom." He sucked in a breath, suddenly feeling like a teenager trying to ask a girl to a dance. Idiocy. He cleared his throat and strengthened his voice. "The cuff links I'm wearing were gifts from the ambassador we're dining with tonight. They'd been in his family for a century. The clasps stick."

Before he could finish, her door opened. She stood before him in a pale blue satin dress. Sleeveless—strapless—it should have given him a delightful view, but she wore a little lace thing over it—sort of a jacket, but not quite long enough.

Her hair had been put up, but not in the grandma hairdo. It was more like a long, silky, braided ponytail with flowers woven through it.

She lifted her pretty face and smiled at him. "Heirlooms, huh?"

He said, "Yes," but his voice came out rusty again. Except this time he knew why he was dumbstruck. She wore almost no makeup, yet she was still the most beautiful woman he'd ever met.

"Let me see."

He held out his arm and she examined the cuff links that he'd slid through the buttonholes but hadn't locked. She took the first in her nimble fingers, her face pinching in concentration, and something warm and wonderful swished through him.

He told himself it was nothing but attraction, but when she finished closing and locking the cuff links, she glanced up and smiled at him, and he realized how nice she was. It was no wonder she was so good with the children of her high school. She was just plain sweet.

And he was a pampered ruler. Somebody so accustomed to getting his own way that he'd persuaded her to marry him. It was for the best, of course, but that was his pathology. Even if it hadn't been the best for Ginny, if it had been the best for his country, he would have tossed her feelings aside and worked things to his benefit anyway.

The warm, fuzzy feeling she inspired shifted into cold, hard steel. Because that's who he really was, and even as much of a bastard as he could be, he didn't want to hurt her.

Not after she was doing so much for him.

Dom and Ginny left their apartment at ten to seven. He was the picture of kingly gorgeousness in his black tux.

When she told him that, he cast a sideways glance at her. "Thank you. You look lovely, too."

Not twenty minutes before they had shared a happy moment over his cuff links. Now he was cool and distant? It didn't make any sense.

They walked to the elevator, which opened as soon as they arrived. Neither spoke as they stepped inside and Dom pushed the button for the second floor.

A guest of the palace, Ginny's mom was invited to join them for dinner, and she waited for them in the second-floor lobby beside the elevator.

When they stepped out, she hugged Ginny. "Very pretty."

Ginny displayed her newfound curtsy skills. "Thanks. Your outfit is gorgeous, too."

Rose smoothed her hand along the soft beige satin. The king had offered the services of their clothier, and her pragmatic mom hadn't had a qualm about using them. She had the tailor whip up a simple satin skirt and sequined top that sort of looked like a tank top. She'd swept her yellow and pink hair into a neat French twist. She looked simple, but elegant. More elegant than Ginny had ever seen her.

As Dom guided them in the direction of the king's quarters, Rose whispered, "I could get used to this."

Ginny's eyes widened in horror. She had no idea why Dom had suddenly become distant, but hearing her mom say she could get used to luxury wouldn't help things.

"Do not say that!"

"I was kidding! It's stuffy here." She glanced around at the paintings on the elegant walls. "Almost like a really fancy prison."

Though Dominic hadn't appeared to have been listening, he turned and said, "Protocols and security are necessary."

"For protection and respect," Ginny quickly told her mom, wanting Dom to see her mom hadn't meant any harm. She simply wasn't up to speed on the lives of royalty. "If somebody's going to rule a country in a part of the world that isn't always stable, they need to command respect."

Dominic gave her a look of approval that helped alleviate the sense that she'd somehow caused his bad mood.

But her mom waved a hand. "Give me the good old-fashioned life of a commoner any day of the week."

Ginny smiled nervously, as Dom shook his head. He'd been so cute when he'd come to her suite, asking for help with his cuff links. Now a world of distance seemed to be lodged between them. She wouldn't tell him, but it had been nice to have a chance to touch him. And there was nothing more intimate than fixing a guy's cuff links or his bow tie—as a wife would.

She told herself not to go overboard with those thoughts and knew she wouldn't. She didn't want to get hurt by spinning fantasies. Still, though she might be a fake fiancée about to be a fake wife/princess, she and Dom were in this together. She didn't like the fact that he was unhappy. Especially if it might be because of something she'd done.

Security guards opened the gold doors to the king's quarters and Dom invited Ginny and her mom to enter before him. The foyer ceilings had to be three stories high. Everything from lamps to picture frames was trimmed in gold.

Her mother immediately recognized a Monet. She gasped. "Oh, this is delightful! One of my favorites."

"I'd be happy to give it to you as my wedding gift to you."

All heads turned as the king entered the foyer.

He kissed Ginny's hand, then Rose's.

Rose frowned. "First, I do not have the kind of security I'd need to put that in my home. Second, I'm not the bride. I don't get gifts."

"It's our custom to give parents of people who marry into our family a gift…something like a welcome to the family."

Her mom's eyebrows rose as she glanced over at Ginny, who shrugged slightly.

She leaned toward the king and whispered, "We're really not going to be in your family long."

He bowed. "A custom is a custom."

Rose nodded. "Point taken. Do I have to get you a gift?"

King Ronaldo unexpectedly smiled. "Do you wish to welcome me to your family?"

Rose laughed noisily. "Well, honey, I guess I do. Except you have to come to my house to get the gift."

The king directed everyone to the door again. "Maybe I will. But right now we're going to the formal reception room to meet the ambassador."

The king took Rose's arm as Dominic tucked Ginny's hand in the crook of his elbow.

She'd never seen her mom flirt. Not even after her dad had died. Not with anyone. Ever. The sight of her mom and the grouchy king—well, flirting—made her want to say, "Aw," and shiver with revulsion simultaneously.

King Ronaldo peeked over his shoulder at Ginny. "By the way, Ginny, I approve of the dress."

"This old thing?"

He smiled patiently. "I know you're coming to understand our customs and our etiquette, so you can't tease me anymore by pretending you don't understand. Were I you, I would have said thank you."

Dominic gave her a look and, suddenly, desperately wanting to please him, she took a quick breath and said, "Thank you."

"I'm hoping your entire wardrobe and wedding apparel will follow a similar pattern."

"Yes, Your Majesty. I appreciate that you're allowing me so much say in the wedding plans."

"Thank your future husband," the king said as the reached the door of the reception room. "He pleaded your case. Something about pink roses and your friends as bridesmaids lending authenticity to the whole thing."

Two guards opened the doors. The king walked into the room and led her mother to a discreet bar.

Ginny turned to Dom. "So, you pleaded my case?"

He glanced back at his father. "Saving an argument."

She reached up and tightened his bow tie. "Well, I appreciate it."

He caught her hand. "That's fine. My tie is fine."

She nodded quickly, annoyed with herself for the intimate gesture and for upsetting him again. "I guess I'm just getting a little too comfortable with you."

He caught her gaze. "You shouldn't."

Ginny stared into his dark, dark eyes, suddenly realizing he wasn't angry with her. But if he wasn't angry with her, that left only himself. Was he angry with himself? For asking her for help with cuff links? Or because asking for help with his cuff links proved they were getting close? Becoming friends?

She saw that as a good thing. Within the cocoon of their conspiracy, for the first time in her life, she was taking the initial steps of trusting a man. She didn't have to worry about consequences. There were none. She knew they were getting divorced. There was no way he could hurt her. And the little bit of intimacy with the cuff links had been warm and wonderful.

But obviously, he didn't feel the same way.

The ambassador arrived and Ginny played her role exactly as Dom wanted her to play it. They had a toast with the ambassador and his wife, Amelia, who then toasted the newly engaged couple and wished them happiness.

The ambassador then handed them a small box. Dominic opened it, smiled and handed it to her.

She glanced inside and her gaze jerked to the ambassador. "Emerald earrings."

Amelia said, "Our country's gift to you on your engagement."

She said, "Thanks," but her stomach tightened. She hadn't considered that kings and ambassadors and entire countries would give her gifts. But really? What wedding didn't attract gifts?

At the end of the evening, when the ambassador and his wife retreated to their suite, she and Dom also took their leave. Rose had decided to stay and have one more drink with the king, and Ginny's head spun.

When they got into the elevator and the door closed, affording them their first privacy of the evening, she turned to Dominic. "I don't know if I should apologize for my mom flirting with your dad or groan over the fact that we're going to get expensive wedding gifts that we have no right to."

"We're getting married. We have every right to get gifts and well-wishers have every right to send us gifts." He frowned slightly. "Haven't you seen the stack of presents that have already arrived?"

Her mouth fell open. "We've already gotten gifts?"

"Many. The protocol is that they stay with Sally until she has an appropriate thank-you card printed up on the royal family's stationery."

"We don't write our own thank-you cards?"

He smiled briefly.

Ginny held back a groan. No wonder he didn't want

to be friendly with her. She was more than a commoner. She was a bumpkin.

She swallowed. "What are we going to do with the presents?"

"What do you mean, what are we going to do with the presents? The same thing other newlyweds do."

The elevator door opened and he walked outside. She stood frozen, feeling odd—feeling horrible, actually. While she was learning to trust him, he was walking away from her. She might be a bumpkin, but he was the one who had his protocols out of order if he wanted to keep gifts they didn't deserve. Technically, they were at the center of perpetuating a fraud. They would benefit from a lie.

She scrambled after him. "So we're going to keep these things?"

He stopped, spun to face her. "What would you suggest? That we tell our guests no gifts? That we all but let them know we plan on divorcing. Get your head in the game, Ginny!"

His tone was like a slap in the face. She took a step back, then another. "I'm sorry."

He cursed. "Why are you saying you're sorry! I'm the one who just yelled at you! Do you have to be so nice? So honest?"

"You'd rather I be dishonest?"

"I'd rather that your sanctimonious attitude not make me feel like I'm doing something wrong all the time."

He turned to the white double doors, marched over, opened them and walked directly to the bar.

She scampered after him. "Wait! What?"

"You're so nice. You spar with my dad, then say something so respectful, he knows you're coming around. You didn't want a new wardrobe until we insisted. You're nice with Sally. You're happy your mom is here and it's clear she loves you." He stopped, sucking in a breath.

"You're mad at me because the situation is working out?"

"I'm mad at you because every day it becomes clearer and clearer that I'm going to hurt you."

She tilted her head, not quite understanding what he was getting at.

"You say you don't want to get drawn into this life and I believe you. But you and I..." He downed the shot of Scotch and poured another. "We sort of fit. You feel it as much as I do. It's not something we plan or intend to do. It's that thing that happens at odd moments. The times we're on the same page or thinking the same thought and we know it with just a glance." He walked from behind the bar to stand directly in front of her. "And pretty soon we're going to start remembering how good we are together in other ways and then we're going to be sleeping together."

Her heart thumped. He *was* feeling the same things she was. That unexpected trust. That sense that everything was going to be okay. "You thought we were good together?"

"You *know* we were good together."

"And you think we fit?"

"I see those little things happen every day. You liked fastening my cuff links. I like fighting your simple battles over things like jeans versus white suits."

She searched his gaze. Ridiculous hope filled her chest to capacity. They really were getting to know each other and in knowing each other, they were beginning to genuinely like each other.

For once, having more than a surface relationship

didn't scare her. Maybe because she knew it had a time limit. She could get close, make love, get married, have a baby with Dom, knowing it was going to end. Secure in the fact that they would part amicably, she wouldn't suffer the pains of rejection. She would simply move on. And she would have had a chance she never thought she'd get: a chance to really be in love. To know what it felt like to share. To be part of something wonderful. All under the protection of the knowledge that it wouldn't last forever. She didn't have to be perfect forever. She didn't even have to be good forever. Or to suit Dom forever. She only had to make this work for a little over two years.

"And you don't think it's a good thing that we get along?"

"I have a job to do. I've told you that if you get in the way of that job, I will always pick the kingdom over you."

She swallowed and nodded, knowing exactly what he was saying, but her stomach fluttered. When they first decided to marry, he had been sure he'd always take the kingdom's side over hers. But this very argument proved that he was changing. And he clearly wasn't happy about that.

"Is this the part where I say I'm sorry?"

He sniffed and looked away. "Sorry again? Why this time?"

"Because I think I tempt you. I think that's why you're really mad. I think knowing me has made you feel that you'd like to be a real boy, Pinocchio."

"So I'm a puppet?"

"No. I think you'd like the freedom to make up your own mind, to make your own choices, but you're afraid of what will happen to your kingdom."

He caught her gaze. "You make it sound like an idiotic dilemma. But it isn't. We might be a small kingdom but we're an important one." He slid his hand across her shoulder and to her long ponytail. He ran the fat braid through his fingers as if it were spun gold. "One woman should not change that."

Even as he said the words, he stepped closer. He wrapped the braid around his knuckles and tugged her forward until they almost touched, but not quite. The air between them crackled, not with memories of how good they'd been together but with anticipation. If they kissed now, changed the terms of their deal now, the next two years would be very different.

And she wanted it. Not just for the sex. For the intimacy and the chance to be genuinely close to someone, even as she had the magical out of a two-year time limit.

He lowered his head slowly, giving her time, it seemed, to pull away if she wanted. But, mesmerized by the desperation in his black eyes, she stood perfectly still, barely breathing. He wanted this, too, and even though she knew he was going to kiss her, she also knew he fought a demon. He might want to be king, but he also wanted to be a man.

When his lips touched hers, she didn't think of that night two months ago, she thought of this moment, of how he needed her, even if he didn't see it.

She slid her arms around his neck as he released her braid, letting it swing across her back. With his hand now free, he brought her closer still. The press of her breasts to his chest knocked the air out of her lungs as his lips moved across hers roughly.

He was angry, she knew, because she was upsetting his well-laid plans. The irony of it was he'd been upsetting her plans, her life, from the second she'd met him. It only seemed fitting that finally she was doing the same to him.

Standing on tiptoe, she returned his kiss, as sure as he was. If he wanted to talk about unfair, she would show him unfair. The only way she could be intimate with someone was knowing she had an out. The inability to trust that her dad had instilled in her had crippled her for anything but a relationship that couldn't last. She wouldn't share the joy of raising children. She was lucky to get a child. She wouldn't grow old with someone. The best she would get would be memories of whatever love, intimacy, happiness they could cobble together in the next two years. And even as it gave her at least slight hope, it also angered her mightily.

They dueled for a few seconds, each fighting for supremacy, until suddenly his mouth softened over hers. His hands slid down her back to her bottom, while his mouth lured her away from her anger and to that place where the softness of their kisses spoke of their real feelings.

Like it or not, they were falling in love.

And it wasn't going to last.

But it was all Ginny Jones, high school guidance counselor from Texas with the alcoholic dad, was going to get in her lifetime.

So she wanted it. She wanted the intimacy, the friendship, the secrets and dreams.

The only problem was she had no idea how to go about getting any of it.

CHAPTER SEVEN

IT TOOK EVERY ounce of concentration Dom could muster to pull away from Ginny. He'd never before felt the things he felt with her, but that was the problem. He'd never experienced any of these things because he'd avoided them. Not because he'd never met anyone like Ginny, but because he'd always been strong.

So when he stepped away, it wasn't with regret. It was with self-recrimination. He did not want what she seemed to be offering. And if they didn't stop this idiotic game, just as he'd told her, he was going to hurt her.

"I'm going to bed. I'll see you in the morning." He turned and walked to his room, vowing to himself that something like that kiss would never happen again.

The next day, he left before breakfast and didn't come back to his quarters until long past time for supper. That worked so well he decided to keep up that schedule.

At first, she'd waited for him on the sofa in the sitting room. So he'd stride into the room, barely glancing at her, and walk right past the bar, saying, "It was a long day. I'm going to shower and go right to bed."

And pretty soon she stopped waiting up.

For two weeks, he managed to avoid her in their private times and keep his distance when they were in public, but he could see something going on in that crazy head of hers. Every time they got within two feet of each other, she'd smile so prettily she'd temporarily throw him off balance. But he'd always remind himself he was strong. And it worked, but he wasn't superhuman. If something didn't give, they'd end up talking again. Or kissing. Or just plain forming a team. And then she'd get all the wrong ideas.

A week before the wedding, her bridesmaids arrived and he breathed a sigh of relief. Jessica and Molly were two teachers from her school, both of whom had just finished their semester. Dom smiled politely when Ginny introduced them and he shook both of their hands, reminding them they had met when he visited their school.

Molly laughed. "Of course, we remember you. We didn't think you'd remember us."

He smiled briefly. "It's my job to care for a country full of people. Remembering names, really seeing people when I look at them, is part of that."

Jessica nodded sagely as if she totally understood and agreed, but his future bride tilted her head in a way that told him she was turning that over in her mind, putting that statement up against other things he'd said.

Good. He hoped she was. Because from here on out that was his main goal. If she wanted to be part of his life, and for the next two years or so she had to be, then she needed not just to hear that but to fully understand it. His country came first. She would be second. And then only for about two years. He did not intend to get personally involved with her. God knew he'd sleep with her in a New York minute if he could be sure nothing would come of it. But that ship had sailed. They were getting to know each other, getting to *like* each other. If they went any further, their breakup would be a disaster.

He turned and walked out of the apartment, on his way to his office, but Molly stopped him. "Aren't you going to kiss your bride goodbye?"

Dom slid a questioning glance to Ginny. Her eyebrows raised and her mouth formed the cute little wince she always gave when she had no defense. Obviously, she hadn't told her friends their marriage would be a fake. That was good news and bad news. The good news was if her friends believed this marriage would be real, there was no chance either of them would slip up and say the wrong thing. Unfortunately, that meant there was no rest from the charade for him and Ginny.

He walked over and put his hands on her shoulders. For two seconds, he debated kissing her cheek, but knew that would never work. So he pressed his lips to hers lightly and pulled back quickly, then he turned and walked out to the door.

"I'll be busy all day. You ladies enjoy yourselves."

Then he left. But the look on Ginny's face when he'd pulled away from their kiss followed him out the door. She hadn't minded the quick kiss. She was back to being on board with the charade. Back to fake kisses and no intimate conversations. They'd barely seen each other in two weeks. His doing. And she wasn't pouting. She didn't throw hissy fits the way he distantly remembered his mom doing to manipulate his dad.

He shook his head, wondering where that memory had come from. His mom hadn't been a manipulator. His dad had been brutally in love with her. So in love that the king had been putty in her hands. And so in love that when she got sick and died, the king's world had come to a crashing halt.

Not that he had to worry about that with Ginny. He was much stronger than his dad had been. He could always do what needed to be done. Always resist when he needed to.

With her guests in the palace and a charade to perpetuate, he phoned the kitchen staff and made arrangements for a formal dinner in their apartment, then had his assistant phone Ginny and tell her he was honoring her and her guests that evening with a formal dinner.

Hanging up the phone, Ginny pressed her hand to her stomach. After two weeks of him virtually ignoring her—except when they were in public—he was back to being nice again. She would have breathed a sigh of relief but Molly was two feet away and Jessica wasn't that much farther, standing with the fiftysomething female dressmaker who was measuring her for her bridesmaid's gown.

"So you chose a dress without even consulting us?" Molly groused good-naturedly.

"Yes." Ginny winced. "Sorry, but fabric had to be ordered."

Jessica said, "Oh! Special fabric!"

"It's just a nice silk."

"Listen to her," Molly teased, nudging her shoulder. "A week away from the wedding and she's already acting like a princess."

"I am not!"

Jessica stepped away from the woman who had measured her for her dress. "It's not a bad thing. I imagine that adjusting to being the most important woman in a country isn't easy."

"The most important woman in a country? Not hardly."

Molly fell to a club chair. "Well, Dom's mother is dead and he has no sisters. His dad doesn't date and his brother is some kind of jet-setter. You are the only girl permanently in the mix."

She hadn't thought of that, but when she did, her stomach fluttered oddly. It meant something that they'd brought her into the family. True, she was pregnant with the heir to the throne, but there were so many ways they could have handled this other than marriage. On some level, she'd passed enough tests that they'd brought her in.

"If that makes you queasy," Jessica said, "then you'd better toughen up."

"I'm not queasy."

Molly said, "Well, something's up. You let Dom believe we don't know about your situation. Almost as if you don't trust what he'd say if he knew you'd confided in your friends."

"That's true, Gin," Jessica agreed, slipping on her blue jeans and pretty peach T-shirt that showed off her Texas-girl tan. "If you don't grow a pair with this guy pretty soon, he's going to walk all over you."

"What if I think I have a better way to handle the next two years?"

Jessica cautiously said, "Better?"

"Yeah." She turned away, puttering around with picking up pins and tape measures, and putting them in the dressmaker's tote.

Taking the cue that Ginny wanted her to leave, the dressmaker grabbed her tote and said, "Thanks. I'll have dresses for you to try on tomorrow."

When she closed the suite door behind her, Molly gasped. "Tomorrow?"

She shrugged. "That's how it goes here in the palace." She walked to the table by the window and busied herself with straightening stationery and pens. "I say I want something, somebody comes up and measures, and the next day it's at my door."

Shrewd, Jessica narrowed her eyes. "You never told us your better plan for how to handle your situation."

Ginny looked up into the faces of her two trusted friends and decided it wasn't out of line to want a second opinion. "Okay. Here's the deal. You know how my dad sort of ruined my ability to trust?"

Molly nodded. Jessica crossed her arms on her chest.

"Well, I've been thinking that if Dom and I hadn't accidentally gotten pregnant, I probably never would have trusted anyone enough to have had a child."

Jessica said, "True. So I hope you're not about to tell us you want to make your marriage real with Prince Gorgeous. The very fact that you can't trust makes that just plain stupid."

"Not really. Because I don't want a permanent husband. But I do want this marriage."

Molly tilted her head. "What does that mean?"

"Well, we're stuck together for at least two years and he *is* gorgeous. Not only would I like the whole mother experience with my baby's father, but I just don't see why we can't sleep together and maybe be a real husband and wife for a while."

"How about because that's not what he wants."

"I'll still divorce him two years after the baby's born and gone through the initiation ceremony. That's the deal. But it's the very fact that I know we're getting divorced that makes me comfortable enough to, you know—"

"Want to have sex?"

"It's more than that. When he's comfortable with me,

we have fun. I think we could make very good parents. I think being a husband and wife for real for two years could pave the way for us to have a good relationship after we're divorced and I think all that is nothing but good for our child."

Molly mulled that over and suddenly said, "Actually, that makes sense."

Jessica turned on her. "How can you say that? She's going to get hurt."

Molly shrugged. "Or not. The situation is weird, Jessica. And not everybody's lucky enough to attract men like mosquitoes."

Jessica nodded at Ginny. "She could if she wanted to."

"That's the point. She doesn't want to. But she's going to marry this guy and have his baby. Why shouldn't she have two years of being a real princess before she has to let it all go?"

"That's like saying you should eat a whole cake before you start a diet."

Ginny laughed. "You mean, you don't?"

Jessica groaned.

"Look, I am never, ever, ever going to be married. The mistrust my dad instilled in me will never go away. But I am getting married. To Dominic. For a bit over two years. Not forever. So it'll be like playing house."

Jessica sighed. "Playing house?"

"Yes. Just another facet of the charade. Because I know it's fake, I'm not going to get hurt. But I also want to experience something I never would have if we hadn't gotten pregnant and decided to marry for the baby."

"I hope you know what you're doing."

Ginny sucked in a breath. "I think I do, but even if I don't, it's only two years. Once it's over, it's over. I will have no choice but to go back to normal. Especially with a baby to raise with him." Satisfied with her conclusion, she changed the subject. "Did you bring something to wear tonight, or do I need to call the clothier?"

"Clothier?"

"He's this guy, Joshua, who if you need something you call him, and he'll call a store or designer and have it in the room within hours."

Molly gaped at her. "So you can get us gowns for tonight?"

"If you need them. It's all about not embarrassing Dominic in front of his father."

Jessica shook her head. "I think you're enjoying this too much."

"Actually, this is the part I don't enjoy. The part I won't miss at all. There are lots of things about being a princess like the press and having a father-in-law who can have you deported that make this life hard. Not something I'd want to do forever."

Jessica drew a deep breath. "Okay. Now I think I get it. You know you don't want to be in this life forever, but you like Dom and you're going to make the best of it while you're here. So you'll have no regrets and be ready to move on."

Ginny sighed with relief. "Exactly."

"Okay. Then I'm on board, too. What do you want us to do?"

"Nothing. This is the part I need to handle myself. I just haven't figured out how yet." She couldn't exactly say, "Hey, let's sleep together." But she wasn't the queen of seductresses, either. She was going to have to wait for her moment and take it. Given that he'd managed to avoid her for the past two weeks, that wasn't going to be easy.

They called Joshua, who called his contact at a local boutique from Ginny's suite. Four gowns were delivered within two hours, and Molly and Jessica made their choices before they returned to their rooms to dress for the formal dinner.

Ginny took special care with her outfit that night, wearing a coral-colored gown. She fixed her hair in the long braid again, the way she'd had it the night he'd kissed her.

When she finally came out of her suite, everyone was already there, including her mom—and the king, who was his charming best, and anybody with eyes in their head could see the reason was Rose.

After cocktails, they passed the small dining room where Dom and Ginny ate breakfast and lunch, and entered a much bigger dining room, something almost as fancy as the king's. Dom let the king have the head of the table, taking the seat to his right and seating Ginny next to him.

The conversation ebbed and flowed around them as Ginny watched her mom, seated across from them at the king's right. They talked about everything from sports to politics, and the king took great delight in sparring with her.

"He's going to miss her when she's gone next week."

Ginny's gaze snapped around to meet Dom's. From the surprised expression that came to his face, she could tell he hadn't meant to say that out loud.

"It's okay. You can talk to me. We're a team, remember?" She motioned from herself to Dom. "In this together."

"Yes. But we don't want to go too far."

She turned on her seat, her taffeta gown ruffling and rustling, suddenly wondering if this was her moment.

Everybody at the table was deep in conversation. Her bridesmaids chatted up Dom's brother. The king and her mother were so engrossed, there might as well not have been anybody else at the table.

The best place for her most private conversation with him might just be in this crowded dining room.

She took a breath, caught his gaze. "Why not? We're in a mighty big charade. I think it's going to be impossible for us to set limits on how close it makes us."

"I told you that we don't want to get close because I don't want to hurt you."

"You think you're going to hurt me over a few shared comments? I'm not asking you to divulge state secrets. I'm just saying the charade works better when we're talking." She smiled slightly. "We haven't talked in weeks."

"And it's my fault?"

She shook her head. "Dom. Dom. Dom. You're so uptight. I'm not placing blame. That's the beauty of forming a team and maybe even the beauty of knowing this team doesn't have to last. We're only going to be together for two years or so. After that, we are the parents of your country's next heir who must get along."

Totally against the rules of etiquette, Dom picked up a fork and tapped it lightly against his plate. "So?"

She could think she made him nervous enough to do something out of line. Or she could see she made him comfortable enough to do something totally out of line.

She liked the second. She *believed* the second.

"So, I honestly, genuinely believe that if we would simply allow ourselves to be friendly—maybe even to get close—in these next few years, the rest of our lives would go a lot smoother."

He peeked over at her. "Really? *That's* what you think?"

"Look at it logically. How does it benefit us to never speak? It doesn't. It makes the charade more difficult and opens the doors for us to make mistakes."

"True."

"But if we talk at dinner and lunch, debrief about our days—"

This time when he peeked at her, he sort of smiled. "Debrief?"

"Sally and Joshua are rubbing off on me. I just mean we should talk about our days with each other."

"Ah."

"Then we won't make as many mistakes."

"It seems to me that just a few weeks ago, *you* were ignoring *me*."

"I was figuring everything out."

"And now you think you understand the whole situation?"

"I really do."

"And your answer is for us to debrief."

She met his gaze. "It's more than that."

His eyes darkened. "How much more?"

"I think we need to tell each other our reading interests, where we've been on vacation, a bit or two about our jobs. I think I need to fix your cuff links. You need to let me straighten your tie. I think we should be talking baby names and colors for the nursery."

He held her gaze. "That's going to take us into some dangerous territory."

She took a long breath and with all her strength, all her courage, she kept eye contact. "I'm a big girl. I'm also a smart girl. I sort of like knowing that this relationship will end."

His eyes searched hers. "So you've said."

"My dad was an alcoholic who made promises he never kept. He was his most charming when he wanted to manipulate me. If there's one thing I can't trust, it's people being nice to me. How am I ever going to create a relationship that leads to marriage if niceness scares me?"

He laughed unexpectedly. "You're saying you think a relationship with me will work because I'm not nice?"

"I'm saying this is my shot. Do you know I've never fantasized about getting married and having kids? I was always so afraid I'd end up like my mother that I wouldn't even let myself pretend I'd get married. So I've never had anything but surface relationships." She sucked in a breath. Held his gaze. "This baby we're having will probably be my only child. This marriage? It might be fake to you, but it's the only marriage I'll ever have. I'd love to have two years of happiness, knowing that I don't have to trust you completely, that you can't hurt me because we have a deadline."

"You really don't trust me?"

"I'll never trust anyone."

He glanced around the table at her bridesmaids, who were chatting up his brother, his dad and her mom, who clearly weren't paying any attention to them, and suddenly faced her again.

"No."

CHAPTER EIGHT

THE CATHEDRAL IN which Dom would marry Ginny was at least a thousand years old. It had been renovated six times and almost totally rebuilt once after a fire. The pews were cedar from Israel. The stained glass from a famous Italian artist. Two of the statues were said to have been created by Michelangelo, though no one could confirm it. And the art that hung in the vestibule? All of it was priceless.

But when Ginny stepped inside, her hand wrapped in her mom's, every piece of art, every piece of wood, every famous, distinguished and renowned person seated in the sea of guests, disappeared from Dom's vision.

She looked amazing.

She'd let her hair down. The yellow strands billowed around her beneath a puffy tulle veil. The top of her dress was a dignified lace with a high collar and snug lace sleeves that ran the whole way from her shoulders, down her arms, across the back of her hand to her knuckles. The skirt started at her waist, then flowed to the floor. Made of a soft, airy-looking material, it was scattered with the same shimmering flowers that were embroidered into the lace top, but these flowers stood alone, peeking out of the folds of the fabric and then hiding again as the skirt moved with every step Ginny took.

She'd managed to look both young and beautiful, while pleasing his father with a very dignified gown that took Dom's breath away.

His brother leaned forward and whispered, "I know you weren't happy about this marriage, so if you'd like to trade, you can have your princess back and I'll raise your love child."

Any other time, Dom would have said, "Shut up, you twit." Today, mesmerized by the woman who had already seduced him once, and if he'd read her correctly the night of the formal dinner with her bridesmaids, wanted to seduce him again, he very quietly said, "Not on your life."

Ginny and her mom reached the altar. Rose kissed his bride's cheek and then walked to her seat. Ginny held out her hand to Dom and he took it, staring at her as if he'd never seen her before. Because in a way he hadn't. He'd seen her silly and happy and playful the night of their date. He'd seen her dressed in jeans and T-shirts and even beautifully, ornately, for the night with the ambassador. But today, in this dress that was as beautiful as it was bridal, she was a woman offering herself to a man, as a bride.

Caught in the gaze of her pretty blue eyes, he was floored by the significance of it. Especially after their conversation about making their marriage real for their time together.

The minister cleared his throat. Their hands joined, Dom and Ginny turned to the altar and the service began. As the solemn words and decrees were spoken by his country's highest-ranking religious official, Dominic reminded himself that this wedding wasn't real. Even when they said their vows and exchanged jewel-encrusted rings, he told himself they were words he meant, truly meant, for a limited time.

But when the minister said, "You may kiss the bride," and she turned those big blue eyes up at him, his heart stuttered. She wasn't just a woman in a white dress, helping him to perpetuate a charade that would give legitimacy to Xaviera's next heir. She was an innocent woman, a bride...

She was his now.

She whispered, "You don't want to kiss me?"

His heart thundered in his chest and he realized he'd been standing there staring at her. In awe. In confusion. She wasn't just an innocent. She was someone who'd been hurt. Someone who couldn't trust. If he agreed to make this marriage real, no matter how much she protested that it wasn't true, he would hurt her. He *knew* he would hurt her. Because as much as he hated the comparison, it seemed being royal had made him very much like her dad. He was his most charming when he needed to get his own way, and selfish, self-centered, the rest of the time.

Still, he held her gaze as his head lowered and his lips met hers. He watched her lids flutter shut in complete surrender. Total honesty. His heart of stone chipped a bit. The soft part of his soul, the place he rarely let himself acknowledge, shamed him for being so strict with her.

They broke apart slowly. She smiled up at him.

He told himself she was playing a part. The smile, the expression meant nothing. If she was smart enough to realize she didn't trust anyone, she was also smart enough to play her role well. Smart enough to see he was doing what needed to be done not just for the next heir to the throne, but for *his child*.

The child in her stomach.

They turned to the congregation and began their recessional down the aisle to the vestibule, where they were spirited away to a private room while their guests left the church. They endured an hour of pictures before they walked out of the church, beneath the canopy of swords of his military's honor guard.

Dressed in black suits and white silk shirts and ties, his bodyguards whisked them into the back of his limo, to a professional photo studio for more pictures.

And the whole time Ginny smiled at him radiantly. Anyone who looked at her would assume—*believe*—this wedding was real. Because he was beginning to get the feeling himself. She wasn't such a good actress that she was fooling him. What she'd said haunted him. She wanted this to be real. At least for a little while. Because this, this sham, was as close as she'd ever get to a real marriage.

Her mother rode in the limo with his dad. Her bridesmaids rode with his brother and a distant cousin who served as his best man and groomsman.

Alone in their limo, he turned to her. Struggling to forget the bargain she'd tried to strike and come up with normal conversation, he said, "You look amazing."

She smiled, reached over and straightened his tie. "You do, too."

He shifted away, afraid of her. Not because he worried she was going to hurt him or cheat him. But because he knew she wasn't.

"Dominic, the straightening-the-tie thing is important. A piece of intimacy everyone expects to see. You need to be still and let me do it."

Because of her suggestion that they make this marriage real, and his desperate need not to hurt her, he was now the one who might ruin their ruse. "I suppose."

She shrugged, her pretty yellow hair shifted and swayed around her. "No matter what you decide, I intend to be a good wife for these two years."

His tongue stuck to the roof of his mouth. What did that mean? That he'd find her in his bed that night?

He remembered that yellow hair floating around them their one and only night together, remembered the softness of her skin, and wondered just how a man was supposed to resist that honesty or the sexual tug that lured him into a spell so sweet, another man would have happily allowed himself to be drawn in.

But he wasn't just any man. He was a prince, someday a king. Someone held to a higher standard. He did not deliberately hurt people.

They arrived at the palace. Bodyguards ushered them into the main foyer. They stopped in his father's quarters to have a toast with her mother and his dad and their wedding party. Then they took an elevator to the third floor of his dad's wing of the palace and stood on the balcony, waving to well-wishers.

A young woman edged her way through the crowd to the space just in front of security. She waved and called, "Toss your bouquet!"

Dom said, "That's odd."

Ginny laughed. "She's American. We have a tradition that whoever catches the bride's bouquet will be the next person to be married." She gave him a smile, then winked, before she turned and tossed the spray of fifty roses with strength that would have done any weight lifter proud.

The flowers bowed into a graceful arc before beginning their descent. The crowd gasped at Ginny's whimsy. The people closest to the woman who'd called realized they could intercept the bouquet and they scrambled forward, but it landed in the young girl's arms. As the crowd pressed forward to grab flowers from the bouquet, security surrounded her.

Ginny faced him. "Have her brought up for an audience."

He laughed. "Seriously?"

"Yes." She bowed slightly. "My lord," she said, her eyes downcast, her tone serious.

Those crazy feelings of wanting her rippled through him again. He raised her chin. "You don't have to bow to me."

"The etiquette books say I do." She smiled. "And I'm asking for the wedding favor the book also says I get. I'd like to meet the woman who wants so desperately to be married that she'd risk arrest."

Dom faced his bodyguard. He made a few hand gestures. The crowd called, "Kiss the bride," and he did. But he did so now with curiosity that nudged his fear of hurting her aside. He liked being able to do something for her.

When they returned to the king's receiving room, the young woman awaited them.

Ginny walked over and hugged her. "I hope the whole bouquet thing works out for you."

Their guest laughed nervously. Her big brown eyes stayed on Ginny's face. "I never thought you'd do it."

"I waited years for my prince. I know what you're feeling." She squeezed her hand and said, "Good luck."

Dominic nodded, the security detail motioned her to the door and she left with a quick wave. But the way Ginny had said, "I know what you're feeling," struck him oddly. She didn't say, "I've known what you feel." She said, "I know what you're feeling." He heard the sorrow there, maybe even a loneliness that almost opened that soft place in his soul again. But he hung on. He could not let sentiment destroy his plan. He could not become his dad.

Ginny said, "You know crazy people are going to try to steal that bouquet from her. You're going to have to have someone escort her to her hotel and maybe even out of the country."

"Yes. Security will take care of it."

But he couldn't stop staring at her. He might have closed the soft place in his soul, but his brain was working overtime to figure her out. What she had done had been a tad reckless, but it was very Ginny. Very sweet. Very warm. She'd used the wish her groom was to grant her for someone else.

And *that's* why he knew he couldn't sleep with her. No matter what she said or did or how she phrased things, she was innocent. Too nice for him.

But she was also hurting. She really believed she'd always be alone.

He couldn't think about that. He had to be fair.

They received dignitaries for hours. Even Dom was tired by the time his father, brother, cousin and Ginny's entourage escorted them to the palace ballroom.

They entered amid a trumpet blast and after toasts and a short speech by his father welcoming Ginny into the family, they finally ate.

Still, in between dances, he managed to find time to speak to his detail and arrange for their luggage to be taken to the yacht that night, instead of the next morning.

There was no way in hell he was taking her back to

his apartment, where they'd not only had privacy, they'd had friendly chats and a wonderful kiss.

Even he had his limits.

The staff on the *Crown Jewel* was too big to be in on the marriage ruse, but precautions were easier there. He and Ginny would be sleeping in the side-by-side bedrooms of the master suite, but the yacht was also so big that he could keep his distance. They'd sail so far out onto the ocean that even long lenses couldn't get pictures. And the staff would rotate so the same people wouldn't see them twice and wonder why they weren't kissing or holding hands.

Not only would this work, but it would be easy.

Piece of cake, as Ginny would say.

When they had to take a helicopter to the yacht, Ginny knew why Dom had chosen it as their honeymoon spot. The pilot put the helicopter down on the landing pad, and Dom helped her out, gathering the skirt of her gown so she didn't trip over it as she navigated the steps.

Walking across the deck, under the starlit sky, she glanced around in awe. "It's the friggin' Love Boat."

He turned to her with absolute horror in his eyes. "What?"

"You never saw the television show from the eighties? *The Love Boat?*"

Clearly relieved that she was referencing a television show, not referring to something about their relationship, he said, "You weren't even born in the eighties, so how did you see it?"

"My mom watched reruns all the time. It's a show about a cruise ship."

His eyes narrowed. "So you're saying our yacht is big?"

"Your yacht is huge."

"If that's a compliment, I accept it."

It wasn't a compliment. She was telling him she knew his plan. He intended to use this big ship to avoid her for the two weeks they were to be away. But he didn't seem to catch on to what she was saying.

It didn't matter. She was happy to have figured out his plan. She'd thought the night of the formal dinner for her friends had been her moment, and when it turned out that it wasn't, she'd hoped her honeymoon might give her another shot. And here she stood on a boat big enough to rival an aircraft carrier. It meant her options for finding another moment were seriously limited. But at least she knew what she was up against.

A security guard opened the door for them and Dom motioned for her to enter first. She stepped inside, expecting to see stairs with metal railings painted white, expecting to hear the hollow sound of a stairwell. Instead, she entered a small lobby. Sleek hardwood floors led to an elevator. Gold-framed paintings hung on the walls.

She spun around to face Dom. "Seriously? Is that a Picasso?"

Dom said, "Probably," as the elevator door opened. She hadn't even seen him press a button for it.

They rode down, only a few floors, before the door opened again onto a room so stunningly beautiful it could have been in a magazine. Huge windows in the back displayed the black sky with the faint dusting of stars. A taupe sofa flanked by two printed club chairs sat in front of a fireplace. The accent rug that held them all in a group was the same print as the club chairs. A long wooden bar gleamed in a far corner. Plants in elaborate pots converted empty space into focal points.

She wanted to say, "Wow," but her chest hurt. Her knees wobbled. This was her wedding night. But unlike a normal bride who knew what to expect, every step of her journey was a mystery. She wanted one thing. Dom wanted another. And only one of them could win.

Security guards entered behind Dom, rolling the cart carrying their luggage. She'd packed her four bags with care. Even though Dom had told her she'd need only a bikini and some sunblock, she'd brought clothes for romantic dinners—and undies. Pretty panties, bras and sleepwear that she and Joshua had chosen from catalogs so exclusive that prices weren't listed beneath the descriptions.

Joshua had said, "If you have to ask the price, you can't afford it."

And at that point she decided she didn't want to know. Dominic could afford to buy and sell small countries. She wasn't going to quibble over the price of the nighties she'd probably need to seduce him.

The bodyguards disappeared down the hall with the luggage cart carrying their bags.

"Nightcap?"

She pressed her hand to her tummy. "I probably could use some orange juice."

He walked to the bar. "Tired?"

Was he kidding? Even if she was exhausted, nerves would keep her awake tonight. The last time they'd been in this position, she hadn't had to seduce him. They'd seduced each other. Which meant, she shouldn't be nervous. She should be herself.

Pushing the empty luggage cart, the bodyguards left with a nod to Dom.

And suddenly they were alone.

Straightening her shoulders, she faced him with a smile. "You know what? I think I'll just go change."

She glanced down at her beautiful wedding dress. It would now be cleaned and pressed to be put on display in the part of the palace open to tourists.

"It seems a shame to take this off."

"It is pretty." He smiled. "You were a stunning bride."

Her spirits lifted. No matter how strong he was, he liked her. He'd always liked her. She could do this.

She walked back down the hall to the room she'd seen the guards take their bags and found herself in another sitting room. She shook her head. "These people must spend a fortune on furniture."

The tulle underskirt of her gown swishing, she turned to the right—the side of the suite her room was on in the palace—and headed to that bedroom. She opened the door on another sitting room, this one smaller, and walked into the bedroom, only to find it empty. She glanced in the walk-in closet, thinking they might have carried her bags the whole way in there, but that was empty, too.

She walked out of the bedroom, through the small sitting room, then the big sitting room and to the hall. "Dom?"

He ambled to the front of the hall where he could see her. "What?"

"My stuff's not in my room."

"It has to be. I saw the bodyguards carting it back."

"Well, it's not here."

He huffed out a sigh. "Let me see." He walked back along the hall and through the sitting room into the second bedroom of the master suite. Doing exactly as she had done, he frowned when he didn't see her bags in the bedroom, then checked the closet.

"That's weird."

"Yeah."

He slowly faced her. "They might have put your things in my room."

"Oh?"

"Don't get weird notions. My instruction was for your things to be put in your room." He went into the master bedroom.

On impulse, she followed him. Nothing ever really went as planned with the two of them, so maybe the thing to do would be let things happen.

His room didn't have a sitting room. The big double doors opened onto an enormous bed. Beige walls with a simple beige-and-white spread on the bed gave the room a soothing, peaceful feel. But Dom didn't even pause.

"No luggage here," he said, finding the bedroom empty. He turned to the walk-in closet. He opened the grand double doors and sighed. "And there's everything."

"They think we're sleeping together."

"I told them we're not."

"You actually told them?"

"I told them this marriage is a show for the heir."

"Oh."

"Don't be embarrassed. I'm the one who should be embarrassed. This is my mess we're cleaning up."

"Oh, yeah. Every woman loves it broadcast that her new husband doesn't want her."

"It wasn't broadcast. A few key servants know the secret. It's why we're on the yacht, not at the villa. There are many servants here, and they rotate. None of them is going to see us enough to put it all together."

Suddenly weary, she decided this was not a seduction night. It was a total bust. How on earth could she seduce a guy who had told his servants his marriage was a sham? She turned to leave but stopped and faced him again.

"You know how we did that thing with the cuff links?"

He cautiously said, "Yes."

"Well, there are a hundred buttons on the back of this dress, most of which I can't reach. Can I get some help?"

His relieved "Sure" did nothing to help her flagging spirit. If anything, it made her feel even worse.

Just wanting to get this over with so she could race out of his room, go to her room and be appropriately miserable, she presented her back to him.

His fingers bumped against the first button. She felt it slide through the loop. When it took a second for him to reach for the next button, she realized her hair was in the way and she scooped it to the side, totally revealing the long row of buttons to him.

"That's a lot of buttons."

Holding her hair to the side, she said, "Exactly why I need help."

He quickly undid three or four buttons, then she felt his fingers stall again.

"Getting tired, Your Majesty?"

"No. I'm fine."

But his voice was pinched, strained.

Another two buttons popped through the loops.

"You're not wearing a bra."

"Didn't want the straps to show through the lace."

He said, "Ump."

Another two buttons popped. Then two more. But when his fingers stalled again, she felt them skim along her skin. Not a lot, just a quick brush as if he couldn't resist temptation.

When he got to the last buttons, the three just above her butt, his hands slowed. When the last button popped, she almost turned around, but something told her to be still. His fingers trailed up her spine until he reached the place where he could lay his hands on the sides of her waist. He grazed them along the indent to her hips, then back up again. When they reached her rib cage, they kept going, under her dress to her naked breasts.

Her breath caught. She wanted to tell him she was his. That she'd been his from the moment she laid eyes on him. But she knew this wasn't as easy a decision for him as it was for her.

"You are temptation."

She turned, letting the top of her dress fall as she did so. "I don't intend to be."

"Liar."

She shrugged. "Maybe a little." She raised her gaze to his. "But would it be so, so terrible to pretend you like me?"

He shook his head, as he lowered it to kiss her. Their mouths met tentatively, then she rose to her tiptoes and pressed her lips against his strongly, surely.

She might not get forever. But she wanted this two years enough that she was willing to reach out and take it.

He cupped his hand on the back of her head and dipped her down far enough that her dress slithered around her hips. When he brought her back up again, the dress fell to the floor.

"No panties, either?"

She stood before him totally naked. No lies. No pretense. When she whispered, "It was actually a very heavy dress." He laughed.

Another woman might have worried, but Ginny

smiled. Part of what he liked about her was her ability to make him laugh. She wasn't surprised when he slid his arms around her back and knees, and carried her to the bed.

CHAPTER NINE

GINNY AWAKENED THE next morning with Dom's arms wrapped around her waist. She squeezed her eyes shut, enjoying the sensation, then told herself she had to get her priorities in line before he woke up.

They hadn't talked the night before. They'd had an amazing time, but they hadn't spoken one word. She hadn't been expecting words of love, but she knew making this marriage real hadn't been what he wanted. Though she hadn't actually seduced him, which had been her plan, he could still be upset that he hadn't been able to resist the temptation of their chemistry.

She opened her eyes to find him staring down at her. "Hey."

"Hey." He searched her eyes. "I hope you know what you're doing."

And pragmatic Dom was back.

So she smiled at him and stretched up to give him a kiss. "I do."

"I'm serious about not wanting this to last and about us not getting emotionally involved with each other."

"I hate to tell you, but I'm pretty sure raising a child together will more than get us emotionally involved."

"I'm not talking about being friendly. I'm talking about being ridiculously dependent."

Even as he spoke, he rose from the bed. With the fluidity and ease of a man comfortable with who he was, he stretched and reached for a robe.

She sat up, almost sorry he was covering all those wonderful muscles when he secured the belt around his waist.

He picked up the phone and, without dialing, said, "Bacon, eggs, bagels, croissants, and the usual fruit and juices."

He hung up the phone and walked into the bathroom.

Ginny stared after him. The man really was accustomed to getting everything he wanted. But constantly seeing the evidence of it was a good reminder that he wasn't going to be persuaded to do anything, be anything, other than what he wanted.

He came out of the bathroom, took off the robe and to her surprise climbed back into bed. He leaned against the headboard and reached down to catch her shoulders and bring her up beside him.

Bending to kiss her, he said, "We have about ten minutes before breakfast gets here. Any thoughts on what we should do?" The sexy, suggestive tone of his voice told her exactly what he wanted to do.

She laughed. "I think I need to eat and get my strength back."

He sobered suddenly. "You know, we rarely talk about your pregnancy. Are you okay? Really?"

"Millions of women have babies every day. I'm not special or in danger because I'm pregnant."

"You're pregnant with an heir to a throne." He looked away, then glanced down at her again. "And even if he wasn't heir to the throne, he's *my* baby."

He said it with such a proprietary air that her heart stuttered and she realized something unexpected. "So, like me, if we hadn't accidentally gotten pregnant, you wouldn't have had a child, either."

"No. A baby was part of the deal with the princess of Grennady. But this is different."

"I know." She ran her hand along her tummy, which was no longer flat. Though only slightly swollen, after a little over three months, it was beginning to show signs of cradling a child. "Do you think we're going to be good parents?"

"I don't know about you but I'm going to be an excellent father."

She laughed. "Conceited much?"

"I am going to be a good father," he insisted indignantly. "I know every mistake my father made with me and my brother—especially my brother—and I won't do those things." He shifted against the headboard. "What about you?"

"My mother was aces as a mom." She laughed. "Still is. My dad left a lot to be desired."

"So you're not going to drink?"

She shrugged. "I sometimes think it's smarter to demonstrate responsible behavior than to avoid something tricky like alcohol."

"Whew. For a while there I thought you were going to tell me I was going to have to give up drinking until our kid was in college or something."

Thinking of all the times she'd seen him come to the apartment and head directly to the bar, she turned slightly so she could look him in the eye. "It wouldn't hurt you to cut down. Maybe not drink in the afternoon."

"My job is stressful."

"Scotch isn't going to take that away."

"But it makes me feel better."

She peeked up at him again. "Really?"

He shrugged. "Some days. Others not so much. Those days it's better to keep a clear head."

"You deal with some real idiots?"

"Most of the people in our parliament come from old oil money. They care about two things. Keeping their families wealthy and keeping our waterways safe so that they can keep their families wealthy."

She laughed. "You're making fun, but it makes sense."

"Right after my mother died there was a problem with pirates."

"Pirates!" For that, she sat up and gave him her full attention. "I love pirates!"

He gave her a patient look. "These pirates aren't fun like Jack Sparrow. They're ruthless. Cutthroat. There was a particularly nasty band all but making it impossible for tankers to get through without paying a 'fee' for safe passage. The papers exploded with criticism of my dad for not taking a firm hand. Parliament called for his resignation. And he sat in his quarters, staring at pictures of my mom, having all his meals brought up, not changing out of sweats."

"Holy cow." Entranced now, she shimmied around to sit cross-legged on the bed so she could look directly at him as he spoke. "What happened?"

"On the last second of what seemed to be the last day before he would have been required to face down parliament, my dad sent the military to destroy the pirate ships. It was a war that lasted about forty-five minutes. He bombed the boats until there was nothing left but smoke and an oil slick."

"Wow."

"Then he sent the military to the country that was

aiding and abetting, and just about blew them off the map."

Two raps sounded on the door. Dominic pulled away. "That would be breakfast. You wait here."

"You're bringing me breakfast in bed?"

He tilted his head. "It looks like I am."

She saw it then. Not just his total confusion over his feelings for her, but the reason for it. He'd said before that his dad had made a mistake that he did not intend to repeat. This was it. Except she couldn't tell if the mistake was grieving his dead wife or being in love with his wife so much that he'd grieved her.

Dominic returned, rolling a cart covered with a white linen tablecloth into the room. He pulled a bed tray from beneath the cart and said, "I'm about to put bacon and eggs on this tray, so get yourself where you want to be sitting."

Still cross-legged in the middle of the bed, she patted a spot in front of her. "I like to be able to look at you when we talk."

"So you're going to want me to take off the robe while we eat?"

She pointed to herself. "I'm not dressed."

"You're certainly not dressed to receive company. But I like you that way."

The warmth of his feelings for her sent a shudder of happiness through her. He put the tray on the bed in front of her, lifted a lid from a plate of food and set that on the tray.

He motioned to the cart. "There's a variety of juices, pastries, toasts, fruit. What else would you like?"

"Just a bottle of water."

One of his eyebrows rose. "No fruit?"

"Oh, so suddenly you're not so unhappy with me eating fruit."

"I wasn't unhappy that you were eating fruit the day you fainted. I was unhappy that you seemed to be eating only fruit. You and the baby need a balanced diet."

Her spirits lifted again. She liked talking about the baby as a baby, not the next heir to Xaviera's throne. She patted her tummy. "I know exactly what to eat."

Though Dom took three calls after they ate and while Ginny showered, he couldn't shake the glorious feeling that he really didn't have to do anything for two whole weeks.

When she came out of the bathroom, dressed in a pretty sundress, he caught her shoulders and kissed her deeply before he pulled away and said, "I love the dress, but why don't you slip into a bikini and we'll sit on the deck and get some sun?"

She smiled cautiously. "Okay."

Unexpected fear skittered through him. "What's wrong?"

"Honestly, I have no idea what we're supposed to be doing."

"We can do anything we want, which is why I suggested sitting on the deck, getting some sun. I haven't had a vacation in a long time and just sitting in the sun for a few hours sounds really nice."

She bounced to her tiptoes and brushed a quick kiss across his mouth. "Bring a book."

He laughed. "I'm not *that* unaccustomed to taking a break."

"Good." She turned to go back into the bathroom/ dressing room, closet area.

Needing to get dressed himself, he followed her.

She stopped in front of a rack of clothes—her clothes—that now hung there. She frowned. "Did you unpack for me while I showered?"

"No. Servants must have done it. There's an entrance in the other side of the closet. Obviously, they came in, did what needed to be done and left."

She turned slightly and smiled at him. "So your privacy isn't really privacy at all."

"I have minions scurrying everywhere."

He meant it as a joke, but his comment caused her head to tilt. That assessing look came to her face again, but he took it as her trying to adjust to everything.

He was glad for that. Two years was a long time, and she'd need to be acclimated to everything around them—around him—in order to be casual in public.

Honesty compelled him to say, "You really won't get much in the way of privacy."

She smiled. "Do you think a guidance counselor in a school with two thousand kids ever gets privacy?"

He laughed. "At home." He winced. "At least I hope no one bothered you at home."

"It was never a bother to have someone contact me at home. If one of my kids thought enough to call me or come by, it was usually because they were so happy about something they wanted to share." She raised her gaze to meet his. "Or they were in trouble. And if they were, I wanted to help."

"That sounds a heck of a lot like my job. But multiply your two thousand by a thousand."

She nodded. "That's a lot of people."

He said, "All of them depending on me," then watched as she absorbed that.

"That's good for me to know."

"And understand. These people depend on me. I will not let them down."

As easy as breathing, she slid out of the sunny yellow dress and, naked, lifted a bikini out of one of the drawers.

He'd seen her naked, of course; they'd spent the night making love and the morning talking on his bed. What was odd was the strange sense of normalcy that rippled around him. He'd never pictured himself and the princess of Grennady sharing a dressing room. Even if they made love, she'd be dressing in the suite across from his, if only because she was as pampered as he was. Her wardrobe for a two-week cruise wouldn't have been four suitcases. It would have been closer to ten.

But Ginny was simple. Happy. And so was he. Not with sex. Not with the fact that living as a man and wife for real would make the ruse that much easier. He was happy with the little things. Breakfast in bed. The ability to be honest. Dressing together for a morning that would be spent reading fiction.

It was the very fact that these things were so foreign to him that grounded him to the reality that he shouldn't get used to them. In two years all this would be gone.

For the first time, he understood why Ginny had campaigned to make this marriage real. They'd never, ever have this again. He'd be a divorced prince, eventually king, who'd take mistresses while he ran a country and raised a son. And she'd be the king's ex-wife, mother of the heir to the throne.

"You know it's really going to be hard for you to get dates after we divorce."

She turned with a laugh. "Excuse me?"

"Nothing." He walked back to the section of the

dressing room that held his clothes and pulled out a pair of swimming trunks. He couldn't believe he'd thought of that. What she chose to do when they separated was her business. But he knew it might be a good thing for *her* to start thinking about that. Not just to remind her that this wasn't going to last but to get her realizing the next stage of her life wouldn't be easy.

They spent a fun, private two weeks on the yacht, with Dom called away only three or four times for phone calls from members of parliament. Otherwise, he'd been casual, restful and sexy.

When the royal helicopter touched down on the palace grounds, Dom and Ginny were greeted by the whir of cameras and a barrage of questions from reporters who stood behind the black iron fence surrounding the property.

Stepping out of the helicopter, helped by Dom, who took her hand to guide her to the steps, she smiled at the press.

"You look great! Very suntanned!"

She waved at them. "Don't worry. I used sunblock."

The reporters laughed.

Dom said, "We had a great time."

Ginny watched the reporters go slack jawed as if totally gob smacked by his answer. Then she realized they weren't accustomed to him talking to them outside of the press room or parliament.

As they walked to the palace behind bodyguards dressed casually in jeans and black T-shirts—with leather holsters and guns exposed—she turned to him. "That was kind of you to talk to them, Your Majesty."

He sniffed. "I'm rested enough that I threw them a bone."

She laughed. "You should rest more often."

They reached the palace. A bodyguard opened the door and they stepped into the cool air-conditioned space.

She took a long breath of the stale air. "I miss the ocean."

He dropped a quick kiss on her lips. "The yacht is at your disposal anytime you want."

"Are you trying to get rid of me?"

"No." He stopped walking and caught her hand. He kissed the knuckles. "No."

When their gazes met, she knew he thought the same thing he did. Two years would be over soon enough. But she couldn't be happy, be herself, make this relationship work, if it was permanent. And neither could he.

They'd been granted a very short window of time to be happy, but two years of perfection was a lot more than some people got.

So she raised herself to her tiptoes, kissed his cheek and said, "Go visit your dad. Get the rundown on what happened while we were away and I'll be waiting for you for supper tonight."

CHAPTER TEN

THEY SETTLED INTO a comfortable routine that was so easy, Dominic forgot this was supposed to be difficult. Dressing for the royal family's annual end-of-summer gala, he held out his arms to Ginny as naturally as breathing and she locked his cuff links.

"I heard your mother made it in this afternoon."

Ginny glanced up at him, then shook her head. "She didn't want to miss too much class time, so she only took two days off. Your father sent the jet and she got here about an hour ago. She almost got here too late to dress because she keeps forgetting that we're seven hours ahead of her."

He grunted. "She'll get used to it."

Her tummy peeped out a bit when her dress flattened against it as she turned to walk away. He caught her hand and spun her to face him again, his hand falling to the slight swelling. "What's this?"

She laughed. "I thought the flowing dress would hide the fact that I'm starting to show."

Emotion swelled in his chest, but he held it back, more afraid of it than he cared to admit. "You shouldn't hide it. Everybody's waiting to see it."

She groaned. "Everybody's waiting to see me get

fat? Thanks for the reminder that I'll be getting fat in front of the world."

He grabbed his jacket and motioned her out of their bedroom. "That's one way of looking at it. The other is to realize that since everybody's so eager to see you gain weight, you now have full permission to eat."

She stopped and pivoted to face him. "Oh, my gosh! I never thought of it that way. For the next five months I can eat on camera."

"Subjects will love seeing you eat on camera."

She rubbed her hands together with glee. "Bring on the steaks."

He opened the apartment door and led her into the echoing foyer. "Should I tell them to give you two from now on?"

She inclined her head. "Might not want to start big. I should work my way up to the second steak."

They entered the elevator. As it descended she slid her arm through his. The door opened and they made their way to his father's quarters, where her mother was holding court. He thought it odd for the real royal, his dad, to be letting Ginny's mom monopolize the conversation. Still, he walked into a room to the sound of his brother laughing and his dad trying to hide a laugh.

"Mother, please tell me you're not telling off-color jokes."

Rose gasped at the sound of her daughter's voice. When she turned and saw the same thing Dom had seen that evening—the slight evidence of a baby bump— her eyes misted. She raced over and put her hands on Ginny's tummy.

"Oh, my gosh."

As she had with him, Ginny groaned. "Great. Just great. Everybody's going to notice."

"Subjects are eagerly waiting for this," Dom's father said, sounding happier than Dom had ever heard him.

"That's what I told her." He nodded to the bartender to get him a Scotch but stopped midnod and shook his head. He didn't need a drink. Didn't want a drink. Not out of respect for her sensitivity because of her dad's alcoholism. But out of a sense of unity. This child was both of theirs, but technically she was doing all the work, all the sacrificing. He walked to the bar, got two orange juices in beautiful crystal and handed one to Ginny.

Alex laughed. "You're drinking orange juice?"

He glanced at his brother's double Scotch. "Maybe I'd like to have a clear head in case we go to war?"

"Bah. War!" The king batted a hand. "That miserable old sheikh who's been threatening had better watch his mouth."

Ginny spun to face him. "A sheikh's been threatening?"

"Rattling his saber." Dom took a sip of his orange juice.

She stepped back, tugging on his sleeve for him to join her out of the conversation circle. "Is that what the orange juice is about?"

He looked at the glass, then at her and decided to come clean. "No, as my dad said, the sheikh is just being an idiot. I realize you're doing all the heavy lifting with this pregnancy. I thought I'd show a little unity, if only in spirit."

"Oh." She kissed his cheek. "Now, there's something you should tell the press."

"Are you kidding?"

"No. If they like baby bumps, they'll love hearing that you're sacrificing your Scotch."

"This sacrifice isn't permanent. It's only for tonight."

"Still, it's charming."

"Oh, please. It took me decades to lose the Prince Charming title. I'd rather not go there again." He pointed at his brother. "Alex lives with it now."

"Still…" She sucked in a breath and caught his gaze. "Thank you."

He displayed the glass. "It's a little thing. Not much really." Yet he could see it meant a lot to her, and knowing that gave him a funny feeling inside. Add that to his ability to see her baby bump every time she shifted or moved and he couldn't seem to take his eyes off her.

His father led them to the ballroom, where they entered to a trumpet blast. After an hour in a receiving line, he noticed Ginny looked a little tired and was glad when they walked to the dais. His father made a toast. As minister of finance, he gave a longer toast.

The press was escorted out as dinner was served and, relieved, Dom sat back. Watching Ginny dig into her pork chops with raspberry sauce served with mashed potatoes and julienned steamed carrots, he laughed.

"You're going to be finished before I get three bites into mine."

"Everyone said pregnancy would make me hungry all the time. They should have said ravenous."

He chuckled.

She eyed his dish. "You got a bigger serving than I did."

"Wanna switch plates?"

She sighed. "No."

"Seriously. I'll save some. If you're still hungry you can have it."

"I'm gonna get big as a house."

"In front of the whole world," he agreed good-naturedly. But when she was done eating, he slid a piece of his pork to her plate. "I don't want you to faint from hunger while we're dancing."

But as he said the words, he got a funny sensation. A prickling that tiptoed up his spine to the roots of his hair. He glanced to the left and right, not sure what he was looking for. He saw only dinner servers in white jackets and gloves. People milling about the formal dining room.

Calling himself crazy, he went back to the entertainment that was watching his wife eat and didn't think of the prickling until he and Ginny were on the dance floor an hour later. With everyone's attention on his father and Ginny's mother, who were doing their own version of a samba, he felt comfortable enough to enjoy holding Ginny, dancing with her. He'd spun her around twice, then dipped her enough to make her laugh, and there it was again. A tingling that raced up his back and settled in his neck.

Still, he didn't mention it to Ginny. They danced and mingled with the dignitaries invited to their annual gala, including the sheikh currently giving them trouble.

She curtsied graciously when introduced. "I was hoping you could settle your differences tonight."

The sheikh's gaze bounced to Dominic's. Dominic only shrugged. She hadn't really said anything *too* bad.

The sheikh caught Ginny's hand and kissed it. "We don't talk business at the gala."

She bowed apologetically. "I'm so sorry. But since I was hoping that settling this agreement might get me two weeks on the yacht with my husband I guess I didn't see it as business."

The sheikh laughed. "I like a woman who doesn't mind asking for what she wants."

Ginny smiled. Dominic took the cue and said, "Perhaps we could meet first thing Monday morning."

"If your father's schedule is free."

"I'm sure it will be for you."

An hour later, seeing that Ginny was tired, Dominic excused himself to his father who—along with Ginny's mother—thought it was a good idea for her to leave.

He took her hand and led her down a few halls to their elevator. When they were securely behind the door of their apartment, he tugged on her hand and brought her to him for a long happy kiss.

"You do realize you just accomplished what diplomacy hasn't been able to get done in three weeks."

"Does this mean I get my three weeks on the yacht?"

"I thought it was two."

"I want three."

"You're getting greedy."

She curtsied. "I just like my time with you, Your Majesty. And your undivided attention."

He scooped her off her feet and carried her to their bedroom. "I'm about to give you all the undivided attention you can handle."

The next morning Ginny awakened as she had every day since their marriage, wrapped in his arms. At six, Dom rolled out of bed and used the bathroom. He slid into a robe and, from seeing his daily routine, Ginny knew he'd gone to their everyday dining room. Sliding into a pretty pink robe, Ginny followed him.

"Not sleepy this morning?"

Rather than take her chair, she slid to his lap. "I feel extraordinarily good."

"So maybe we should do what we did last night every night."

"Maybe we should."

The sound of the servant's door being opened brought Ginny to her feet. As she walked to her side of the table, a young girl wheeled in a cart containing his breakfast of bacon and eggs, plus bowls of fruit, carafes of fruit juices, and plates of pastries and breads.

She smiled at Ginny expectantly. Knowing she was waiting for her breakfast order, Ginny said, "I'll just eat what we have here."

Dom glanced over. "No bacon? No eggs?"

"Wait until you see now many bagels I eat."

He laughed as the serving girl left.

As always, their meal was accompanied by fourteen newspapers. She grabbed *USA TODAY* as he took London's the *Times.* Their table grew quiet until Dom flipped a page and suddenly said, "What?"

Busy putting cream cheese on a bagel, Ginny didn't even look over. "What's the *what* for?"

He slammed the paper to the table and reached for the house phone behind him. "Sally, get up here."

Ginny set down her bagel. "What's going on?"

He shoved the paper across the table. She glanced down and saw a picture of her and Dom with their heads together as their dinners were served, a picture of her and Dom dancing, a picture of Dom leading her out the back door of the ballroom. All beneath the headline: The Affectionate Prince.

"At least they didn't call you Prince Charming."

He glared at her.

"Dom, I'm sorry. Your picture gets in the paper almost every day here in Xaviera. I'm missing the significance of this."

"First, no press is allowed in that ballroom once dinner starts. So one of our employees got these pictures."

As the ramifications of that sank in, she said, "Oh."

"Second, look at that headline."

"'The Affectionate Prince'?" She caught his gaze. "When you want to be, you are affectionate."

"No ruler wants to be thought of as weak."

"Weak? It's not weak to love someone." Instantly realizing her mistake in saying the *L* word, Ginny shot her gaze to his. For a few seconds they just stared at each other, then he bounced from his seat, almost sending it across the room.

"This was exactly what I didn't want to happen!"

Ginny said, "What?" not quite sure if the unexpected anger coursing through her made her bold or if she was just plain tired of skirting the truth. "Are you mad that your happiness shows? Or are you really that surprised or that angry that we fell in love?"

"I can't love you."

"Oh, really? Because I think you already do."

There. She'd said it.

Their gazes met again, but this time his softened. He took his seat again. "Ginny. I can't love you."

Since she'd already made her position clear, she said nothing, only held his gaze.

"My dad loved my mother."

"Oh, damn him for his cruelty."

"Don't make fun. When my mother got sick, my dad slipped away, let our country flounder because he was searching the globe for someone, *something* that could save his wife."

"And you think that was weakness?"

"Call it what you want. Weakness. Distraction. Whatever."

"How about normal human behavior?"

"Or a lack of planning."

"You think your dad should have had a contingency plan in case his wife got sick?"

"I think he let pirates get a foothold because he put my mother first."

"Oh, Dominic, of course he put his sick wife first."

He shook his head as if he couldn't believe what she'd just said. "A king cannot put anyone ahead of his country. At the first sign of those pirates he should have involved the military."

"Even though his wife, the woman he obviously adored, was dying? How could he have avoided scrambling to save her?"

His gaze rose until it met hers. "By not falling in love in the first place."

Something fluttered oddly in her stomach. The conversation was making her sick and sad and scared. But the feeling went away as quickly as it came. "I see."

"The stakes of this game, my life, are very high, Ginny. We don't govern or rule our people as much as we protect them. I can't afford a slip, a lapse." He combed his fingers through his hair. "When I'm king I won't get two private weeks on a yacht. I'll get vacations that include video conferencing and daily briefings. I'll get two hours, at most, in the sun. A twenty-minute swim." He sucked in a breath. "And this is why I warned you. Even if I wanted to love you. Even if I fell head over heels for you…coming in second to a country isn't like being second to a hobby. You would get very little of my time. It wouldn't be worth loving me."

Stunned, Ginny watched him toss his napkin to the table. "Where is Sally?"

Then he stormed out of the dining room because he didn't have anything to give her.

And that was the truth he'd been trying to tell her all along.

CHAPTER ELEVEN

GINNY SAT STARING at her bagel when there was a knock on the apartment door. She expected it to be Sally, so when her mom walked into the dining room and said, "I thought we were going to swim this morning," Ginny dropped her bagel to a plate.

"I'm not much in the mood."

Her mom took a seat, grabbed a Danish pastry and popped a bite into her mouth. "First fight?"

"You know this isn't a real relationship."

"Oh, sweetie, of course it is. Get any man and woman involved in a plot or plan of any type and what results is a relationship."

"Yeah, well. It's short-term."

"Why is this bothering you suddenly?" Her eyes narrowed. "You want to change the rules."

Ginny rose from her seat. "I'm in my robe. I need to get some clothes on. Sally's supposed to be coming up."

"Dom was on his way out when he let me in."

"He must have called Sally and told her he would come down to her." She headed toward the bedroom. "I need to get dressed anyway."

She wasn't surprised when her mom followed her out of the dining room and into Dom's bedroom.

Seeing the entire bed was happily rumpled, she faced Ginny. "Well, this is a change of plans."

"You don't really think we were going to be married and not sleep together, Mom." She put her hand on her stomach and the strange flutter happened again.

"Honey, I knew you'd be sleeping together. I just didn't think you realized it would happen." She walked over. "What's up with your tummy? You're not sick, are you?"

"I don't know. I don't think so. But every couple of minutes this morning I've been getting this strange flutter in my stomach."

"Oh, my gosh! The baby's moving!"

"He is?"

"Or she is!" She plopped her palm on Ginny's stomach. "Let me feel." Her eyes filled with tears. "Oh, my gosh. Oh, Ginny. I'm going to be a grandma."

Ginny fell to the bed. "That fluttering is my baby?"

Rose sat beside her on the unmade bed. "Yep." She nudged Ginny's shoulder. "Mama."

She pressed her lips together. "Mama. I'm going to be somebody's mom."

Rose slid her hand across her shoulders. "Yes, you are. And whatever nonsense is going on between you and Dom, you have to straighten it out."

"There is nothing to straighten out. The deal is made. I leave two years after the baby's born."

Rose studied her face. "But you don't want to go now. You love him."

"And I think he loves me, too, but he doesn't want to."

"Oh, what man willingly falls in love?"

Ginny laughed.

Rose said, "Give him time."

"Time won't heal the fact that he thinks love makes a ruler weak."

"Really?"

"You know his mom died, right?"

Rose winced. "Kind of hard not to see that Ronaldo's wife isn't around."

"She was apparently sick for years with cancer." Ginny sighed. "He tried everything to save her and in that time the country fell apart."

"So?"

"So, parliament called for his resignation. Had he not snapped out of it he would have lost his crown."

"Oh."

Ginny rose from the bed and paced to the dresser. "I never realized how difficult their job was."

Her mom leaned back, balancing herself with her hands behind her. "How so?"

"Their location forces them into a position of needing to protect the waterways. While Dom's dad was scrambling to save his wife, pirates began attacking ships, demanding money to pass."

"That's not good."

"The press crucified the king. Parliament called for removal of his crown."

"So you said." She sat up. "But I still don't get how this means he can't have a wife."

"He doesn't want to be weak."

"You know the marriages I've seen that work the best are the ones where a husband and wife form a team."

"If you're suggesting that I should help him rule, you are out of your mind. Not only would he *never* let that happen, but I can't rule. I could make a suggestion or two, but I couldn't rule."

Rose batted a hand. "You're good with people,

sweetie, but not that good." She stood up and walked over to Ginny. "You love this guy."

Ginny didn't even try to deny it.

"So how in the hell could you possibly be willing to let him live this demanding, difficult life alone?"

Ginny blinked.

"You're looking at this from your side of the street, but what about his? Ronaldo told me that his wife was the treasure he came home to at night. That when the world was rocky, her silliness was his salvation. She was beautiful, elegant and could charm the birds out of the trees. But he didn't care about any of that. He liked that she played gin rummy with him until the sun came up on nights he couldn't sleep. He liked that he could talk about anything with her, knowing she'd never abuse the power of his confidences and that no one would ever know she'd heard things that were supposed to be secret."

Rose took a breath and patted Ginny's shoulder. "Do you really think Dom will live much past sixty if he doesn't have a friend, a buddy, a confidante, a lover who's willing to be whatever he wants without making demands?"

"No."

"And can you see the lonely life he'll have unless you try to work this out?"

She sucked in a breath. "Yes."

"Ginny, you always believed that being a guidance counselor was a calling. But what if this is your calling? Not just being Dom's true partner, but also raising your child so that he or she isn't buried under the stress of ruling?"

"Maybe I have been looking at this selfishly."

"Not selfishly, but ill informed. Now that you know

how difficult all this is, you've got to do whatever you can to make Dom's life easier."

Dom and Sally easily found the serving boy who had taken the pictures, but that didn't change the fact that the damage was done. Dom looked at photos of himself on the dais, on the dance floor and leading Ginny to the rear entrance to return to their apartment, and even he saw it—the weakness. The ease with which he stepped out of his role as leader and into the role of what? A smitten lover?

He could not have that. He would not be his dad. If anything, now was the time to prove that he was stronger than his father.

He didn't have lunch with Ginny, didn't return to the apartment until after eight that night. When he opened the door and entered the sitting room, he found her on the sofa, reading a magazine. Dressed in a soft red robe with a floral nightgown beneath it, she rose when she saw him.

"Did you catch the creep who took those pictures?"

He headed for the bar. "Yes."

"Want to talk about it?"

"No."

She returned to her seat. "Okay."

Silence descended on the room. He looked at the Scotch with disgust, remembering the orange juice he'd been drinking for "unity." What was wrong with him that he'd been such a schmuck? All he'd been doing since their honeymoon was giving her the wrong idea.

He set the glass on the bar and didn't even tell her he was going to get his shower. He let the water sluice over him, reminding himself that he was a ruler, royalty, someone set aside to do the noble task of keeping his people safe. He stood in the shower until he began to feel like his old self.

He put on a pair of pajamas and crawled into bed with the latest popular thriller. He might not be a television guy or a movie buff, but he liked a good story, a good book. He read until ten when his eyelids grew heavy. He set the book on the bedside table at the same time that Ginny entered the room.

He wanted to suggest that she go back to her old room, but couldn't quite bring himself to be that mean. Eventually she'd grow weary of him ignoring her and she'd come to the decision on her own.

Soundlessly, she slipped out of her red robe, exposing the pretty flowered nightie. His gaze fell to her stomach, which peeped out every time she moved in such a way that the gown flattened against it. She said nothing. Just crawled into bed.

But she rolled over to him. She put her head on his shoulder and her hand on his stomach.

He resisted the urge to lower his arm and cuddle her to him. This was, after all, part of how he'd get her to see the truth of their situation and go back to her own room. But when her breathing grew even and soft and he knew she was asleep, he let his arm fall enough that he could support her.

Then he laid his hand on her stomach.

He closed his eyes, savoring the sensations of holding her, and fell asleep telling himself that it wouldn't hurt to hold her every once in a while.

Dom's life became a series of long days and empty meals. With Ginny's mom deciding to retire to help Ginny care for the baby, he didn't have to worry if she had company or if she was being cared for or entertained. In fact, the way she slept in in the morning and had lunches and most dinners with her mom made him feel they were establishing a great system for being together without being together.

The thing of it was, though, she was in his bed every night. She never said a word. Didn't try to seduce him. She just rolled against him, put her head on his shoulder and her hand on his chest and fell asleep.

He didn't resist it. Not because he took comfort from the small gesture, but because she was pregnant with his child, and he was hurting her. It almost seemed that this little ritual was her way of easing away from him. And if this was what she needed to do to get through the next months, he would let her have it.

But one night, she rolled against him and something bounced against his side. He peered down. The stomach beneath her thin yellow nightgown looked much bigger when she was on her side.

The bounce hit him again. He stiffened but she laughed.

"That's your baby."

He sprang up. "What?"

"Your baby." She took his hand and set it on her stomach. "He's moving."

The rounded stomach beneath his hand rippled. His jaw dropped. He smoothed his fingers along the silken nightie.

She sat up. "Here." She wiggled out of the nightie and tossed it. Sitting naked in the dark with him, she took both his hands and positioned them on either side of her belly.

The baby moved. A soft shift that almost felt like a wave.

He laughed, but his throat closed. "Oh, my God."

She whispered, "I know."

The desire to take her into his arms overwhelmed him and he pulled her close, squeezing his eyes shut. "Thank you."

She leaned back so she could catch his gaze. "For showing you the best way to feel the baby or for actually having the baby?"

Her eyes warmed with humor. The tension that had seized his back and shoulders for the past six weeks eased and he laughed. "It's a big deal to have a baby."

"Millions of women do it every day."

He sobered. "But not under such ridiculous conditions."

She took his hand, pressed it to her stomach again. "The conditions aren't that bad."

"You're not going to have a life."

She shrugged. "I know. I already figured out it'll take some hellaciously special guy to ask out a woman who's divorced from a king and mother to a child who's about to become king." She met his gaze. "Very few guys will want to get on the bad side of a man who can answer the question 'you and what army?'"

With the baby wiggling under his fingers, he said, "I'm so sorry."

She waited until he looked at her again, then she whispered, "I'm not."

"Then you haven't fully absorbed the ramifications of this mess yet."

"First, I don't think it's a mess. I told you. I didn't think I'd ever become a mom. This baby is a great gift to me." She shrugged. "So I have to give up dating permanently?" She put her hands on top of his. "This is worth it."

"It is."

He didn't mean to say the words out loud. He now hated doing *anything* that gave her false hope. But she smiled and lay down.

"I'm sorry. Are you tired? Do you want to go to sleep?"

"Sleep?" She laughed and pointed at her stomach, which still rippled with movement. "You think I'm going to sleep with the Blue Man Group rolling around?"

He laughed, too, and settled on his pillow again. "Have you thought of names?"

"I pretty much figured your country would name her."

He sat up again and looked down into her eyes. "The country?"

She shrugged. "Parliament." She shrugged again. "Maybe your dad. Maybe tradition."

"Tradition plays a role but essentially we get to name the baby."

Her eyes lit. "Really? So if I want to call her Regina Rose, I can?"

He winced. "Sure."

"You don't like Regina?"

"I'd rather she just be Rose. It's a good solid name."

"It is." She paused a second before she said, "And if it's a boy?"

"I've always been fond of James Tiberius Kirk."

"*Star Trek!* You'd name our baby after someone in *Star Trek*?"

"Not just any old someone. The captain. Plus Tiberius is an honorable name." He met her gaze. "So is James."

"I might not mind it if we dropped the Kirk."

"I think that goes without saying."

He lay down again. She snuggled into his side.

"You know the sheikh still asks about you."

She laughed.

"He wanted to know if you got your three weeks on the yacht."

"Did you tell him I didn't?"

"No."

"Did you explain that we had a fight?"

He sat up again. "This isn't a fight. It's the way things have to be."

She said, "Yes, Your Majesty." Not smartly. No hint of sarcasm and he knew she understood.

It should have made him feel better. It didn't.

He lay back down again. "Have you thought about what you're going to do in two years?" He couldn't bring himself to say *after we divorce*. He knew that would hurt her too much.

"I'm still debating something Sally said about using my notoriety to bring attention to my causes."

"Education?"

He felt her nod.

"You know, you can still live in the palace."

"I know."

That would be hard for her, but having just felt his baby move for the first time, strange emotions coursed through him. He couldn't imagine Ginny gone. Couldn't quite figure out how two people raised a child when they lived in separate houses. He'd been so cool about this in the beginning. So detached. But now that he'd felt his child, was getting to know Ginny, he saw all those decisions that were made so glibly had sad, lonely consequences.

"I just think it would be easier if I lived on the other side of the island. I'd be close, but not too close."

He swallowed, grateful she wasn't taking his baby

halfway around the world. Still, an empty, hollow feeling sat in his stomach. "Makes sense."

She said, "Yeah," but he heard the wobble in her voice. She fell asleep a few minutes later, but Dom stayed awake most of the night. Sometimes angry with himself for hurting her. Other times angry with life. An ordinary man would take her and run with the life they could have together.

But he was a king—or would be someday. He didn't get those choices.

CHAPTER TWELVE

THE FIRST DAY of every month, Dom and Ginny made a public appearance that always included questions from the press. With her eight-months-pregnant stomach protruding, Ginny struggled to find something that wouldn't make her look like a house while Dom attended to some matters in his office.

She finally settled on straight-leg trousers and a loose-fitting blue sweater—knowing it would make her eye color pop and hopefully get everybody's attention on the baby. After stepping into flat sandals, she walked into the living room just as there was a knock at the door. Her mom entered without her having to answer the door.

"You're not glowing today."

"Nope. Why didn't anybody tell me that pregnant women didn't get any sleep when they got close to their due date?"

"Nobody wants to scare women off," her mother said with a laugh as she entered the sitting room. She bent and kissed Ginny's forehead, then sat beside her on the sofa.

"Dom not coming around?"

"Nope. And I'm out of tricks. We talked baby names. I've shown him how to feel the baby move. We eat

breakfast and dinner together every day, and nothing.
I'm out of ideas, short of seduction." She pointed at
her stomach. "And we both know seduction would be
a little awkward now."

"I'm so sorry, sweetie."

"It's fine. But I've gotta run. I get to play loving princess now, while he ignores me."

They left through the front of the palace so long-range
lenses could pick up photos of Dom opening the door
for Ginny.

Every inch of Dom now hated the charade he'd created. It was working, but it was also a strain on Ginny.
When she was just a normal woman, a one-night stand,
he didn't see the strain as being as much of a big deal,
though he knew it was a sacrifice.

But now that he could see the effects of her sacrifice, her swollen stomach, the sadness that came to
her eyes every time she realized how empty, how hollow their relationship was, it burned through him like
a guilty verdict pronounced by the gods. She had been
the sweetest woman in the world, and in spite of the
way he was using her, she was still sweet, still genuine, still helping him.

If he didn't go to hell for this, it would be a miracle.
Because he certainly believed he deserved the highest
punishment.

She slid into the limo and blew her breath out in a
long, labored sigh.

His gaze darted to hers. "Are you okay?"

She placed her hands on her basketball stomach. "I'm
not accustomed to carrying twenty-five extra pounds."
She laughed good-naturedly. "Sometimes I get winded."

The funny part of it was she didn't look bad. Wearing slim slacks that tapered to the top of her ankle and a loose blue sweater that didn't hide her baby bump but didn't hug it, either, she just looked pregnant. Her arms hadn't gained. Her legs hadn't gained. She simply had a belly.

A belly that held his child.

"If the trip is too much, we can go back to the palace."

"Only to have to reschedule it for tomorrow?" She shook her head. "Let's just get this over with."

The guilt pressed down again. He glanced at her feet, pretty in her pink-toned sandals. Her whimsy in the choice of color made him smile.

"You have an interesting fashion sense."

She gaped at him. "I have a wonderful fashion sense, Mr. White-Shirt-and-Tie-Everywhere-You-Go. You need to read *Vogue* every once in a while."

The very thought made him laugh.

Her head tilted as she smiled at him. "It's been a long time since I heard you laugh."

"Yeah, well, our saber-rattling sheikh is back and he isn't the country's only problem. It's hard for me to laugh when I have business to attend to."

Her pretty blue eyes sought his in the back of the limo. "Is it really that difficult?"

He turned his head to the right and then the left to loosen the tension. "Yes and no." Oddly, he felt better. He could twist his neck a million times, sitting in the halls of parliament, and nothing. But two feet away from her and the tension began to ebb.

"Ruling is mostly about paying attention. Not just to who wants what but also to negotiating styles and nonverbal cues. There are parliamentarians who get quiet right before they walk out of a session and spill their guts to the press. There are others who explode in session." He caught her gaze again. "I'd rather deal with them."

She smiled and nodded, and the conversation died. But when he helped her out of the limo at Marco's sea-side coffee shop, she was all smiles.

A reporter shouted, "Coming back to the scene of the crime?"

She laughed. "If fainting was a crime, tons of preg-nant women would be in jail." She smiled prettily as she slid on the sunglasses that made her look like a rock star. "Just hungry for a cookie."

With his bodyguards clearing a path, they made their way into the coffee shop. Standing behind the counter, Marco beamed with pleasure.

He bowed. "It is an honor that you love my cookies."

She laughed. "The pleasure is all mine. Not only do I want a cookie and a glass of milk for now, but I'm tak-ing a half-dozen cookies back to the palace."

Marco scurried to get her order. Dominic frowned. "Don't you want to hear what I want?"

"Hazelnut coffee," Marco said, clearly disinterested in Dominic as he carefully placed cookies in a box for Ginny. Antonella brought Dominic's coffee to the counter.

He pulled a card out to pay, but Marco stopped him with a gasp. "It is my honor to serve our princess today."

Dominic said, "Right."

Because Ginny didn't faint this time, Dom could ac-tually lead her out to the long deck that became a dock. He set her milk on the table in front of her, along with her single cookie. He handed the box of six cookies to a bodyguard.

Ginny said, "There better be six cookies in that box when we get back to the palace."

Dominic's typically staid and stoic bodyguard laughed.

After a sip of coffee, he said, "They love you, you know?"

She unwrapped her big sugar cookie as if it were a treasure. "Everybody loves me. But there's a reason for that. It's not magic. I'm a child of an alcoholic. I *know* everybody has something difficult in their life so I treat everyone well."

"I treat everyone well."

She lifted her cookie. "Yeah. Sort of."

"Sort of? I never yell at anyone. And if I reprimand, it's with kindness."

"You're still a prince."

"Dominic?"

Dom glanced up to see his boarding school friend, Pietro Fonichelli. The son of an Italian billionaire and a billionaire several times over in his own right, thanks to his computer software skills, Pietro was probably better known around the globe than Dominic was. He was also on Dominic's list of friends, the people his bodyguards were told to allow access to him.

Dominic rose. "What are you doing here?"

As he said the words, Dom noticed Pietro wore shorts and a big T-shirt.

"Vacationing." He faced Ginny. "And this is your lovely bride."

It was the first time Dominic was uncomfortable with the ruse. Engaging in a charade to help his subjects enjoy the birth of the country's next heir? That was a good thing. Fooling someone he considered a friend? It didn't sit well. Pietro had been at the wedding, but there had been so many people that at the time it hadn't registered that he was tricking a friend.

He politely said, "Yes, this is Ginny Jones."

Pietro laughed. "Ginny Jones? Is she so American that she didn't take your last name?"

Ginny rose, extending her hand to Pietro. "No. Dom sometimes forgets we're married."

Laughing, Pietro took the hand she extended. Instead of shaking it, he kissed the knuckles.

Something hot and fuzzy whipped through Dom. The custom in Xaviera was that a man had a choice. A handshake or a kiss. He should not be upset that his friend chose a kiss. It was nothing more than a sign of affection for the wife of a friend.

Holding Dom's wife's gaze, Pietro said, "I'm not entirely sure how a man forgets he's married to such a beautiful woman."

Ginny smiled as if she thought Pietro's words were baloney, but Dom had never seen his friend so smitten before. Just as Dom had been tongue-tied and eager the day he'd met Ginny, Pietro all but drooled.

Ginny said, "Dom's a great husband."

"Yeah, well, if he ever isn't—" he let go of Ginny's hand and pulled out a business card "—this card has my direct line on it."

Ginny laughed, but Dom said, "What? Are you flirting with my wife?"

"Teasing," Pietro said. He pulled Dom into a bear hug, released him and said, "It was great to run into you." He glanced at Ginny, then back at Dom. "We should do dinner sometime."

The air came back to Dom's lungs and he felt incredibly stupid. He knew Pietro was a jokester. He knew his friend loved getting a rise out of Dom. It was part of what made them click. They could joke. Tease. "Yes. We should."

With his coffee gone and Ginny's cookie demolished, they walked back to the limo, one bodyguard conspicuously holding a box of a half-dozen brightly painted sugar cookies.

He helped Ginny into the limo, then sat beside her, realizing Pietro was the kind of man who wouldn't care if her ex was a king. He would pursue Ginny. With the money to buy and sell loyalty, her connection to a king would mean nothing to him. Once Ginny was free of Dom, it wouldn't even cross Pietro's mind to care that she'd been his wife. He'd pursue her.

His nerves endings stood on edge like the fur of a hissing cat. *Not out of jealousy*, he told himself. Out of fear for her. Pietro might be a great friend, but he wouldn't be a good husband. Like Dom, he took what he wanted. Discarded it when he was done.

His nerves popped, and he suddenly knew another consequence of this fake relationship. In two years, he was going to have to watch his wife with another man.

That night in bed, the tension that vibrated from Dom rolled through Ginny. She considered shifting away, going to her own side of the bed, but she couldn't. Her baby would be born in thirty-two days, give or take a week for the unpredictability of first babies, and in two short years she would be gone. She wouldn't give up one second of her time with him. Even if it meant she wouldn't sleep tonight because the muscles of Dom's arm beneath her head had stiffened to concrete.

Finally, unable to take the tension anymore, she said, "What's wrong?"

"Nothing."

"Right." Knowing they weren't going to get any sleep anyway, she ran her fingers along the thick dark hair on his chest and said, "So I'll bet it was nice seeing your friend today."

He laughed. "Yeah. Nice."

"You know he was only teasing."

"Yes. He's a jokester and if he'd do something stupid at a bar, the press would love it and it could take the heat off of us."

"I don't mind the heat."

He didn't say anything for a second, then his arm tightened around her shoulders. "I know you don't."

"So we don't need for your friend to get punched out at a bar."

"Especially since I would like to have dinner with him. Actually, he's somebody I'd like to have in the baby's life. He started off wealthy, could have bummed around the world forever on his dad's money, but he knew the importance of being strong, being smart. I might just make him the baby's godfather so he's here for more than the big events."

She nodded but tears came to her eyes as an awful scenario ran through her brain. In two years, she and Dom would be divorced, but Dom and the baby's lives would go on—without her. She would come and go for those big events in the baby's life. She'd even be a part of things, but not really. After her two years were up, she'd be an outsider looking in.

"Are you crying?"

Dom's soft voice trickled down to her.

She swallowed. "It's just a pregnancy thing."

He sat up slightly and shifted her to her pillow so he could look down at her. "Is there anything I can do?"

You could love me, she thought and wished with

all her heart she could say the words. But she'd seduced this guy twice. She'd agreed to his plan to have their child born amid celebration. She was good to his family, good to his employees, good to the press and his subjects. She didn't spend a lot of money, but she did spend enough that she looked like the princess he wanted her to be.

And what did she get for her troubles? The knowledge that in two years she'd be nothing to him.

She sniffed.

Dominic's eyes widened with horror. "Please. Silent tears are one thing. Actually crying will make us both nuts."

"Really? I'm fat. I'm hungry. I'm *always* hungry. I'm always *on*. I've been good to you, good to your family, good to your subjects and you can't love me."

He squeezed his eyes shut. "It isn't that I can't love you."

"Oh, it's just that you *don't want to love me.* That makes it so much better."

He popped his eyes open. "It isn't that, either."

"Then explain this to me because I'm tired but can't sleep. And I'm hungry even though I eat all the time. And I just feel so freaking alone."

"We could call your friends."

"I want my husband."

"The Affectionate Prince."

"I don't give a flying fig what the press calls you. This is our baby. Half yours. You should be here when I need you."

"I am here when you need me."

"Yeah. Right. You're here physically, but emotionally you're a million miles away."

"I rule a country."

She shook her head. "Your dad rules the country. You work for him. Technically you're just the minister of finance."

"I need to be prepared for when I take over."

"Really? Your dad is around fifty-five. He's nowhere near retirement age. You and I could have three kids and a great life before your dad retires."

He laughed. "Seriously?" But she could tell from his tone of voice that the thought wasn't an unpleasant one.

She sat up. Holding his gaze, she said, "Would it be so wrong to ease off for the next ten years?"

He shook his head with a laugh. "First you wanted two years…now you want ten?"

"Yes." A sense of destiny filled her. The this-is-your-moment tug on her heart. There was something different in his voice. He wasn't hard, inflexible, as he usually was. In some ways, his eyes looked as tired as hers.

Could he be tired of fighting?

"I'm asking for ten years, Your Majesty, if your dad retires at sixty-five."

Dom frowned.

She plowed on, so determined that her heart beat like a hummingbird's wings. "What if he works until he's seventy? What if he's like Queen Elizabeth, keeping the throne until he's ninety? We could have a long, happy life."

Dom shook his head. "My dad won't rule until he's ninety." He caught her gaze. "But he could—will—rule another ten years."

"Doesn't ten years even tempt you?"

"You tempt me."

"So keep me. See if we can't figure this whole thing out together? See if we can't learn to have a family—be a family—in ten years."

* * *

It sounded like such a good plan when his heart beat slow and heavy in his chest from the ache of knowing he was about to lose her. He lowered his head and kissed her. Her arms came up to wrap around his shoulders and everything suddenly made sense in Dominic's world.

The buzz of the phone on his bedside table interrupted his thoughts. He didn't want to stop kissing Ginny. Didn't want this moment filled with possibilities to end. So he let the phone go, knowing it would switch to voice mail after five rings, only to have it immediately start ringing again.

The call of duty was stronger than his simple human needs. He pulled away from Ginny with a sigh, but didn't release her. Stretching, he retrieved the receiver for the phone and said, "Yes?"

"One of our ports has been taken by the sheikh. We are at war."

CHAPTER THIRTEEN

DOMINIC DIDN'T JUMP out of bed; he flew. "I don't know how much of this is going to hit the press or how soon, but the sheikh has taken one of our ports. He's telling people we're too weak to protect our waterways, so he's taking over. Which means that port is the first step to all-out war."

Ginny sucked in a breath. On top of all the other odd things she was feeling tonight, having her husband go to war made her chest hurt. She grabbed his arm as he turned to find clothes and get dressed.

"Where will you be? You don't actually have to lead troops into battle, do you?"

"No. There's a war room. My father and I will direct the military from there." He pursed his lips for a second as if debating, then sat on the edge of the bed. "I'll be fine. It's our military who will suffer casualties. Because we don't want to attack our own facility, we have to try diplomacy first. Worst-case scenario happens if he tries to move farther inland or take another port. Then there will be battles, casualties." He caught her gaze. "And then you might not see me until it's over."

She nodded, but the tears were back. No matter how strange or odd she felt, she didn't want to stop him from doing his duty. In fact, there was a part of her that was proud of him.

She leaned forward and kissed him. "Go stop that guy."

He nodded, dressed and raced out of the room.

Ginny lay in bed, breathing hard. Her stomach felt like a rock. Everything around her seemed out of control. So she did some of the breathing she'd been taught in the childbirth classes Sally had arranged for her. Even though Dom was supposed to be in the delivery room, he hadn't attended the classes. But since most of it was about breathing and remaining calm, he really hadn't needed to. Nobody could remain calm and detached the way Dom could.

She breathed again, in and out, and her stomach relaxed. Knowing she wouldn't sleep, she got out of bed and grabbed her book. Sitting on the sofa—with all her lights on because she was just a little afraid, and stupid as it sounded, the light made her feel better—she read until three o'clock in the morning. Her stomach tensed often enough that a horrible realization sliced through her. Still, with weeks until her due date, she didn't want to think she was in labor. So she let herself believe these contractions would pass.

But at seven, she couldn't lie to herself anymore. She picked up the house phone and dialed her mom's extension. "I think I'm in labor."

"Oh, no! Ginny, sweetie…this is too early."

Her stomach contracted again and she doubled over with pain. "All right. I no longer *think* I'm in labor. I know I am."

"Did they tell you what to do?"

"I have to call the doctor, but—" She doubled over again. "Oh, my God, this hurts."

"That'd be labor. Okay. I'm coming over. I'll call Sally who will tell Dom."

"He's in the war room. We're at war."

Her mom was quiet for a few seconds, then she said, "Didn't know if you'd been told, but, yes. I saw the news this morning. We're at war."

"I don't even know if Dom can come out for this."

"Oh, dear Lord, of course, he can. You just go get some clothes on so security can get you to the hospital. I will take care of calling Sally who will get Dom to the hospital."

Ginny did as she was told. The week before she'd been advised by her birthing coach to pack a bag for the hospital "just in case." So after sliding into maternity jeans and a sweater, she lugged the bag from Dom's room to the sitting area.

Then pain roared through her stomach and she fell to the sofa. She tried to breathe, but the fear that gripped her kept her from being able to focus. Her new country was at war and she was in labor. Four weeks too early. She didn't even want to contemplate that her baby might not be ready, but how could she not?

When she was almost at the point of hyperventilation, her door swung open and her mom raced in. "I talked to Sally, who said she will talk to the king. She said not to worry. She'll take care of everything."

She rose from the sofa, the pain so intense, tears speared her eyes again. "Good."

The doors opened again and Dom's top security team ran in.

"Ma'am? Can you walk?"

She caught her mother's hand. "Oh, jeez. Now I'm ma'am."

Her mother led her to the door. "That's right, sweetie. Keep your sense of humor."

Her labor lasted twelve long hours. Every twenty minutes she asked where Dom was. Every twenty-one minutes her mother would say, "He's been told you're in labor. He'll be here any minute."

She gave birth to a healthy, albeit tiny, baby boy. The happy, smiling doctor, a man who'd clearly gotten sufficient sleep the night before, joyfully said, "Can you tell me his name?"

She blinked tiredly. "For the birth certificate?"

He laughed. "No, just because I'm curious."

She swallowed. "We didn't really pick a name yet." But she remembered James Tiberius Kirk. There were some times Dom could be so much fun, so loving, that she *knew* this war had to be god-awful to keep him away from his son's birth.

The doctor placed her little boy, her little king, in her arms, and the tears that fell this time were happy tears. "Look at him, Mom." But she wished she was saying that to Dom. She should be saying, "Look at your son."

But they were at war. And he was needed.

Still, the sting of giving birth to their child alone caused tears to prick her eyelids.

"He's beautiful." Her mom kissed her cheek. "But you're tired."

"Have you heard from Sally?"

"Not a peep."

"Okay."

The doctor walked to the head of her bed. "The nurses need to take your son to be cleaned up and examined. You can have him back in an hour or so."

"You're taking him?" She hadn't been told this protocol, but it just didn't seem right to hand over the future king to people who were essentially strangers.

The doctor laughed and pointed outside the delivery room doors where her security detail stood guard. "Don't worry. He's already been assigned security. He might be leaving your sight but he won't be leaving the royal family's sight."

Her mom took the future king from her arms. "Why don't you go to sleep, honey?"

She said, "Okay," and felt herself drifting off as her mom handed her little boy to the doctor.

When she woke forty minutes later, she took off the ugly hospital gown they'd insisted she give birth in, and with her mom's help put on a pretty nightgown. She prayed Xaviera's war didn't last long, and also knew that when he could Dom would slip out and see his son. She wanted him to see she'd done okay. That she was fine. She was being the stiff-upper-lip princess she needed to be in this difficult time.

Nurses brought her baby back almost exactly an hour after he'd been taken away. The royal pediatrician came in and told her that her son was in good health, but he was small, so a few precautions would be taken.

The pediatrician returned the next morning and gave her the same report. She squeezed her hands together nervously. With her mom there, security outside her door and very attentive nurses, she shouldn't feel alone, but she did. They wouldn't let her see a newspaper so she knew whatever was going on had to be terrible.

She wondered how safe the war room was—how safe the palace was? The sheikh had barrels of money, and money bought weapons and soldiers. She knew very little about Xaviera's army and worried that Dom would have to bomb his own ports.

The next day she noticed security outside her room had been doubled. That's when it dawned on her that she hadn't seen any press. When she got out of bed and looked out her window, the world looked calm. Peaceful. Knowing that everybody in the kingdom was waiting for this baby, it seemed odd that the press wasn't climbing the walls, trying to get pictures.

She asked her mom about it when she arrived for a visit and her mom said the baby's birth hadn't been announced.

She gave Ginny a weak smile. "If anyone knew he'd already been born, he would be a target. The king told Sally he believes it's for the best that this news not yet hit the press."

She swallowed, but her fears mounted. "So things are bad?"

"Actually, things aren't bad at all. The way I understand it, the whole mess involves one port and some hostages. Which is why Sally thinks the king believes it's so important that we protect the baby. He would be the kind of leverage the sheikh needs to get himself out of this mess."

"So it's a standoff?"

"According to Sally, it's hours of drinking coffee and waiting."

Incredulous, Ginny gaped at her mom. "They're waiting, but Dom hasn't been able to get away to see me…to see *his son*?"

"Honey, I wasn't supposed to tell you any of this, but I could tell you were worried and it's not right for you to worry."

She fell back on her bed. "No. It's better for me to feel like a complete idiot."

Her mom fluffed her pillow. "You're not an idiot. Anybody would have worried."

"That's not the part that makes me feel like an idiot. I've been sitting here for three days, waiting for my husband, who apparently doesn't care to show up."

"He's dedicated."

"So is the king, but he's talked to Sally, who's gotten messages to you."

"Have you checked your cell phone? Maybe he's tried to call?"

She gasped. "I never thought to take it. I was in so much pain I just left the apartment."

Her mom pulled out her phone. "I'll call security and have someone bring it over."

That brightened her spirits for about an hour. But when the cell phone arrived and there were no calls, they sank like a rock.

"How could he not care?"

Rose busily, nervously, tucked the covers around her. "I'm sure he cares."

"No, Mom. He doesn't." And it took something this extreme to finally, finally get that through Ginny's head. Her husband did not love her. He probably didn't really love their child. He most certainly wasn't curious about their child, who had been born early and who could have had complications.

But a war came first—

Didn't it?

Not when the war wasn't really a war. When there were stretches of time and waiting. When her husband wasn't even king yet. When there was a king who should be doing the decision making but he had time to call one of his staff—not even a family member.

She got out of bed. "Help me pack my bag."

"Ginny, you can't go home yet! You just had a baby."

"My friend, Ellen, had a difficult birth and was home in forty-eight hours."

"But the baby—"

"Is fine. You heard the pediatrician this morning. He's gained the two ounces he needed to put him over five pounds." She grabbed her suitcase and tossed it to the bed. "If he'd been full-term he probably would have weighed eight pounds."

Her mom put her hand over Ginny's to stop her from opening her suitcase. "You cannot leave."

"The hell I can't. And let them try to stop me from taking my own child." She motioned around the room. "As long as I take the thirty bodyguards, I'm fine."

Rose grabbed her cell phone and hit a speed-dial number.

Ginny snatched her phone out of her mother's hands and disconnected it. "What are you doing? Tattling on me to Sally?"

"Ginny, you can't just leave."

"Mom, this isn't about Xaviera or my baby someday being a king. This is about me knowing that if I don't get out of this country with my baby, I'm going to be stuck here forever with a guy who doesn't love me and a king who thinks he's God." She tossed her mom's cell phone to the bed and took her hands. "I have a baby to protect. I'll be damned if my child will grow up to be a man so stuck to his duties that he can't even see his own babies born or love his wife."

She took a long breath and stared at her suitcase. "To hell with this junk! I didn't want these clothes in the first place."

She poked her head out the door and motioned for the two bodyguards to come inside. "I want a helicopter on the roof of this hospital in five minutes. Then I want flown to the nearest safe airport and one of the royal jets waiting for me there." She sucked in a breath. "I'm going home."

The buzz of the king's cell phone had all heads in the war room turning in his direction. Cell phones had been banned. Too many opportunities for picture taking, voice recordings and just plain dissemination of their plans. In fact, no one but the king had left these quarters.

They slept on cots in a barracks-like room, ate food that was made in the attached kitchen and hadn't had contact with the outside world except through the video feed they stared at.

He missed Ginny. More to the point, he *worried* about Ginny. Something had been wrong the night they came here and he just wanted to fix it. But he knew he couldn't, so maybe it was better that he spend three days cut off from her so he didn't make promises he couldn't keep.

His father walked over to where Dom sat in front of a computer, staring at the feed of the port, feed that hadn't changed in twenty-four hours.

His father sat. "What do you think they're doing?"

"Undoubtedly, trying to figure out how to distance themselves from the sheikh since he seems to have deserted them."

"Should we give them a chance to surrender?"

He caught his father's gaze. There was a look in his eye that told Dom this was a test. A real-life hostage crisis for sure, but a chance for his father to test him.

"I'd say we offer them generously reduced prison

terms for surrender and testimony against the sheikh, and go after the sheikh with both barrels."

"You want to kill him?"

"I'd rather arrest him and try him for this. I think making him look like a common criminal rather than a leader who'd started a war he couldn't finish sends a stronger message to the world."

His dad laughed unexpectedly. "I agree." He bowed, shocking Dominic. "Now what are you going to use to negotiate terms?"

He pointed at his father's cell phone. "This might be appropriate. Except I think we should get hostage negotiators from our police to do that. Once again making it look more like a criminal act that a military one."

"Agree again."

Dom called Xaviera's police commissioner and within the hour the rebels had surrendered, all hostages safe. The sheikh was in hiding, but he was too accustomed to luxury to stay underground for long. Dominic had every confidence they would find him, and when they did, he would stand trial.

The fifty military and security personnel in the war room cheered for joy when they received the call that all rebels were safely in jail.

But Dominic didn't want to stay around for the party. He might not be able to love Ginny, but she was pregnant with his child and not feeling well. He needed to get back to her.

He tapped his dad's shoulder. "I'm going to get going."

"Tired?"

"And I need a shower but I need to see Ginny."

As Dom turned to walk away, his dad stopped him. "Dom, there are a few things you need to know."

Expecting more details or facts about their problem, he faced his dad again.

"Ginny has gone home."

"What? Of course, she's home. She's in the apartment."

"No. She's gone back to Texas." He shrugged. "Some women can't handle war. She got a helicopter to take her to a safe airport this morning and took a jet back to her old hometown."

He gaped at his dad. "She's never mentioned wanting to leave before. She was committed—"

"Like I said, some women can't handle war. We've never been at war when she was with us."

"This is absurd. This was hardly a war. It was an ill-conceived attempt to take over our country by a guy who we clearly gave too much credit to."

"She didn't know that."

"How could she not know that! It's been all over the papers!"

"We weren't letting her see the papers."

"What! Why?"

"Because she had the baby the first day we were in here."

This time, Dom fell to a chair in disbelief. Absolutely positive he had not heard right, he looked up at his dad. *"She had the baby?"*

"Yes."

His kept his voice deceptively calm as he said, "And you didn't think to tell me."

"Duty comes before family."

Anger coursed through him. "But I notice you had your phone."

"I did."

"You talked to staff."

"Quite often. I had to keep track of the baby. Because he was born too soon, he was small. They monitored him. I made decisions."

The anger in Dom's blood went from blue to white hot. *"You made decisions."*

"You were at war. And duty comes before family."

Dominic bounced from his chair and punched his father in the mouth so hard the king flew into the wall behind him.

Fifty military men and ten bodyguards drew their weapons.

His dad burst out laughing. He waved his hands at the military and bodyguards. "Stand down."

But nobody dropped his weapon.

Not giving a damn about the sixty-plus guns trained on him Domini roared, "You think this is funny!"

"No. I think it's about time."

He grabbed his father's collar and yanked him off the floor.

"Dominic, you're the one who's always said duty comes before family."

"So you kept my baby from me!"

"I was showing you that what you were doing with your life was wrong. What you thought you wanted didn't work." He calmly held Dom's gaze even as Dom tightened his hold on his collar. "I'd tried hundreds of things over the years to get you to see that you couldn't live the life you had all planned out. I thought Ginny would break you. When she couldn't and the sheikh took our port and then Ginny went into labor, I saw a golden opportunity."

Dominic cursed and squeezed his eyes shut.

"I loved my wife, your mother. And I was neglectful of my duties but I never dropped them the way you were so sure I had. All those months, we were in private negotiations, trying to avoid a confrontation with the pirates, trying to keep from going to war. Because of your mother's death, they did get a few extra weeks. But in the end, I didn't attack until I knew it was the right thing to do. Loving somebody didn't make me weak. Your mother's love made me strong. And you're a fool if you think you can do this alone."

"So you took my baby from me, made Ginny go through labor and childbirth alone."

"For years I'd been talking to you and for years you've ignored me, treating me like somebody who only deserved respect because I had a title. I had to do something drastic or know you would ruin your life."

He released his dad as if he were poison he didn't want to touch.

"Maybe the lesson I learned, Father—*Your Majesty*—is that I no longer want to be connected to you."

His dad very calmly said, "Go after, Ginny. Bring the baby home."

"And then what? Let you torture him the way you tortured me and Alex?"

"When you see the lesson in this, you're going to apologize. Not just for hitting me but for not trusting me."

Dom sincerely doubted it.

CHAPTER FOURTEEN

GINNY'S CONDO HAD long ago been sold. And because her mom had decided to move to Xaviera for the two years Ginny would live there, her mom's house had also been sold. But the new owners hadn't taken possession yet, so that was the sanctuary Ginny targeted. Unfortunately, when her bodyguard unlocked the front door, they found two women and a man, packing her living room lamps.

"Excuse me, this house has sold."

Ginny patted her baby's back. "I know. It was my mom's. It doesn't close for a few weeks. Until then I can use it."

"Your mom hired us to sell the furniture."

"Well, I'm sure by next week I'll have my own house and you can do that. Until then, the house is mine."

The tall woman looked ready to argue, but when she looked at Ginny with her twelve bodyguards and very tiny baby, she sighed.

"Fine." Disgruntled, the two women and one angry man headed for the back door, clipboards in hand.

Ginny turned to Artemus, the leader of her detail. "I don't even know if there's food in the house."

"I have credit cards. I'm authorized to get you anything you want."

"Really? I ran away with the next heir to the throne and they're feeding me?"

"Yes, ma'am."

She glanced around at the small house that wouldn't sleep herself and twelve bodyguards. Plus, she didn't have a crib. And she was beginning to feel bad about taking the baby from Xaviera before Dom even saw him.

Worse, she missed Dom.

She wondered if her rash decision hadn't been caused by postpartum depression, but reminded herself that her husband hadn't wanted to see his child. He'd never loved her, didn't want to. And he planned on bringing their child up to be just like him. She couldn't let that happen.

Still, that didn't mean this was going to be easy.

"This is a mess."

Artemus agreed. "Yes, ma'am."

Just as her mother said, she hadn't really thought this through. But she had to forget about everything except setting up a household. She'd worry about Dom, what she would say to him, how she'd keep her baby safe from his ridiculous rule, when she had the house set up with beds and food.

"I guess I should feed the baby and get on the phone to find a crib."

Artemus nodded. "And I'll send two guys out for groceries."

She took the baby into her mother's small bedroom, breast-fed him and then made a bed for him out of a drawer from her mother's dresser. With the baby secure, she went online and ordered a crib to be express delivered the next day, along with linens, baby clothes, diapers and some sweatpants and T-shirts for herself. Then she started exploring the real estate sites, looking for a house. The baby woke up twice and she fed him once, changed him the other time. Artemus came in and offered her food, but she refused it. She couldn't eat until she got at least something in her life settled.

Dom showered on his father's private jet. Taking the plane had been another way he'd vented his anger, but though he was bone tired he couldn't sleep in the luxurious bed.

Even after a few hours for his dad's duplicity to sink in, Dom still wanted to punch him. He couldn't believe his father had treated Ginny so cruelly, but unexpectedly realized *he'd* been treating Ginny cruelly all along.

And what would he have done while she was in labor? Coached her? Helped her? Or held himself back because he didn't want to give her false hope? He'd have ruined that moment for Ginny every bit as much as his father had ruined it. Maybe more because she'd see him there, but feel the distance between them, the tangible reminder that he didn't want her in his life.

Which was a lie.

He did want her in his life. The feeling of fury that thundered through him when he realized what his father had done hadn't just shocked him. It had been so pure, so total that Dominic hadn't had a chance to mitigate it. In that moment of blazing-hot anger that resulted from white-hot pain, he knew what it was like to miss out on something so important he couldn't even describe it.

His father was right. Dom never would have felt this if his dad hadn't orchestrated it. He'd have covered, hidden, pretended, postured—whatever it took to fool himself into believing he was fine.

But faced with the raw truth of having those moments snatched away from him—he felt it all. The pain. The loss.

And he knew that pain, that loss, that horrible empty feeling truly was the result of the life he'd built.

He also knew that if he wanted Ginny back, all he had to say was that his bastard father had kept him from seeing the baby's birth, from being with her, and he'd be free in her eyes. She loved him. She'd believe him. She'd take him back with open arms.

He fell to the corner of the big, big bed in the outrageous jet that he could use because he would someday be a king.

The only problem was his dad was right. Even if he'd known his baby was being born, he wouldn't have rushed to Ginny's side. He might have seen the final few minutes of the baby's birth. But even then he would have raced back to the war room.

But what his father had done hadn't just opened his eyes. It had changed him. And he didn't want Ginny to take him back on something that wasn't quite a lie, but was a way to get out of being honest.

He had to be honest with her. He wouldn't even hint that she should come home—that he intended to love her—if he didn't know for sure he wouldn't hurt her again.

And that he couldn't promise.

After hours of combing through real estate sites, Ginny heard Artemus enter her room again. Staring at the computer screen, she said, "How big of a house should I get? I mean, should there be rooms for all of you or does the crown pay for separate quarters for you?"

"We pay for separate quarters."

Hearing Dom's voice, she spun around on her seat.

His chin and cheeks bore dark shadows, evidence that he hadn't shaved in days. His eyes looked pale and hollow from lack of sleep—even though he'd just had a ten-hour flight, which was perfect for catching up on sleep. But the killer was that he wore jeans and a T-shirt.

The desire to tease him almost outweighed the desire to jump into his arms and weep. Except this was the man who didn't love her. Who hadn't thought enough of her to come out of a bunker when apparently he could have. Who hadn't been with her for the birth of their child.

This was also the man she'd have to fight for their child. If he thought he'd just fought a war, he was in for a rude awakening because she was about to show him what real war was.

"Get out."

He peered beyond her to the bed, where their son lay in the bottom drawer of her mom's dresser. "Is that my son?"

His voice was soft, reverent.

She tensed her face to stop the muscles from weakening or tears from forming in her eyes. She would not be weak in this fight. Her child would not grow up afraid to love.

Still, they might ultimately get into a battle over this child, but Dom also had a right to see his son.

"Yes. That's our baby."

He caught her gaze. "You didn't name him."

"I didn't think James Tiberius Kirk was your final answer."

He laughed. She didn't.

He took a few steps closer to the bed. "Oh, my God. He's so little."

She had to fight the tremor of emotion that ripped through her at the awe in his voice.

"You would know that if you'd been there for his birth."

He took another step toward the bed. "My father didn't tell me you were in labor."

That sucked the air out of her lungs. "What?"

He paused and faced her, preparing to answer her, but her heart ached for him. His ridiculously pompous dad had kept his baby from him? She saw the anguish on his face. Knew there might be bigger reasons he hadn't shaved, hadn't slept and suddenly wore blue jeans and a T-shirt.

She rose from her chair, took the baby out of the drawer and watched his little face scrunch as he woke. "Hey, little guy, here's your daddy."

She presented the child to Dom and he stared at him. "Wow."

"Yeah, wow." She smiled. "Hold him."

"He's just barely bigger than my hand." He caught her gaze. "Won't I break him?"

She laughed. "I'm going to trust you to be careful." She nudged the blanket-wrapped baby to him. "Put your one hand under his bum and the other under his head."

Dom did as he was told and took the baby. He bent and pressed a kiss to his forehead. Ginny stepped back, unable to handle the sweetness of the meeting anymore. Or Dom's confusion. He was so new to the baby business that it would have been fun to watch him learn and grow with the baby—their baby. But even though his dad had kept the news that she was in labor from him, he'd always said the kingdom would come first. And they'd just lived the reality of what that meant.

She deserved better than that. Her baby deserved better than that.

He caught her gaze. "My dad said something about complications."

"He was just small, so they monitored him."

"You know his birth hasn't even been announced."

"No. Not at first. Eventually my mom told me."

"It seems my dad was teaching me a lesson."

The pompous old windbag.

"I'd always said the kingdom came first. I'd said I'd never love anybody." He glanced over at her. "I said I wouldn't do what he did when my mom died. Apparently that insulted him. So when the war and you going into labor just sort of happened, he saw it as a chance to show me what my attitude really meant."

"Oh." So maybe the king wasn't so much pompous as interfering. Not good, but at least not god-awful. She wanted to ask Dom if he'd learned anything. But he looked so sad and so broken. And she didn't want to soften to him.

"I missed the birth of my son."

"If you'd known I was in labor, would you have come out of that bunker? In those first hours before you knew the threat wasn't as bad as you and your dad had believed...could you have come out?"

"I'd have pushed it." He unexpectedly hugged the baby to him. "I'd have given instructions for the hospital to let me know when you were close—"

"So you might have missed it anyway?"

"Maybe."

His honestly hit her like the swell of an ocean wave. The king might have kept the news from him, but he probably would have stayed away anyway. "Well, that certainly shines a light on that."

"That's why my dad's lesson was such a good one. I had to see what it felt like to have all my choices taken away from me. When I thought…knew…he was behind my not seeing the baby's birth, I felt the unfairness of it and ridiculous anger. But flying over on the plane, I realized what I just told you. That I might have pushed it back and put it off until I missed it by my own doing. I would have been disappointed but I would have made those crazy royalty excuses about duty, and I'd have forgiven myself. I had to experience it this way to feel the real loss."

He met her gaze again. "It gave me a totally new perspective."

Her heart jumped a bit. "So you're going to be a good dad?"

He laughed. "Yes."

And suddenly her war with him lost some of its oomph, too. Even as his changing attitude made her glad for their baby's sake, it also made her very sad. Very tired. Technically, she and Dom were back to where they were when they made this silly deal.

She said, "That's good," but her heart absolutely shattered. She'd have loved to have raised her baby with this Dom.

"Can you forgive me?"

"For missing the baby's birth? Since it means you're going to be a better dad? Yes." She tried to smile but just couldn't quite do it.

"What about for the other stuff?"

"Like…" The man had been sweet and kind. Attentive in a way that might not have been romantic, but he'd been good to her the whole time they were together. He'd always told her he didn't want to fall in love. She was the one who'd pushed. "…what?"

"You wanted me to love you."

Oh, great. Just what she wanted to talk about again. How he didn't love her.

"It's okay."

"Not for me. If you decided you don't want me to love you anymore, I'm in real trouble, because I realized flying over that ocean that I've probably always loved you."

Tears stung her eyes. "Really? Because I've told you that."

He chuckled. "I know you did. But just like the lesson my dad gave me, I sort of needed to lose you—lose everything—before I could realize what I had."

He laid the baby in the makeshift bed. "We're putting a future king in a dresser drawer."

She tried to laugh but a sob came out. He walked over and enfolded her in his arms. "I am so sorry."

She wanted to say, "That's okay," but she couldn't stop sobbing. She'd been alone for days, making decisions she didn't want to make, trying to get food in a house that was way too small. And she'd missed him. And felt betrayed. Alone.

He let her cry until her sobs became hiccups. Then he whispered, "Shouldn't you be in bed, too?"

"I'm fine."

"Right. Just like you were fine right before you fainted in front of poor Marco." He shifted the baby drawer to one side of the bed and pulled down the covers. "Come here."

She did. He helped her lie down, took off her shoes, pulled the covers to her chin and she fell into her first sound sleep in days.

When she woke, it was to the sounds of her son crying.

Dom lay beside her on the bed, watching her. "I think our son wants to be fed."

"Sounds like."

"We are going to have to name him sometime."

"I'm starting to think of him as Jimmy."

"He'll be King James…like in the Bible."

"Better than captain of the starship *Enterprise*."

She slid out of the bed, got James from his drawer, opened her shirt and began to nurse.

Some of the strain appeared to be gone from Dom's face. "You napped?"

He stretched and said, "A bit."

"Do we have to go home right away?"

His eyes leaped to hers. "You're coming with me?"

"We are raising a king together."

"Yes, we are."

"And your dad is nuts with his rules and his tests."

"I think he's going to let us alone with the tests."

"Yeah, wait until you see the dress I'm going to have made for his next formal dinner. He's not the only one who can push people's buttons. Except this time I owe him."

He laughed and for the first time in days, Ginny felt normal. She nudged her head, indicating he should join her and the baby. "Come watch."

"Really?"

"Sure. He's cute. It's fun to watch him eat like a little horse."

Dom scooted down the bed and looked at their baby suckling. He waited a few seconds, then his gaze rose to meet hers. "There is one thing we haven't sorted out."

She smiled. "What?"

"I love you."

She closed her eyes, savoring the words, then she laughed. "You already said that."

"Yes, but I wanted to say it by itself. You know…so you get the real meaning."

She laughed again. And the quiet, two-o'clock-in-the-morning world of Terra Mas, Texas, righted itself.

EPILOGUE

THE DAY GINNY and Dominic returned from Texas, the baby's birth was announced in the papers. It was reported that he'd been born in the time of crisis for the country, and to keep him safe, his birth had been concealed. Most of their subjects had agreed that keeping his birth a secret had made sense. Others yammered on and on about it on talk radio.

Ginny didn't care. Her life was perfect. She just wanted one more promise from her husband.

Rolling Jimmy into a tiny onesie, she said, "This is our last lie."

Dom pulled his sweater over his head before he said, "It isn't a lie. Technically, Jimmy *was* born in an insecure time for the country. Technically, my dad *had* been working to keep him safe. Technically, I *had been* too involved to leave to witness his birth."

"Now you're stretching things." She picked up the baby and he cooed with delight. "I think he likes these pj's."

Dominic put a quick kiss on her lips. "Or he likes his mom."

"He'd better. It'll take me decades to get my figure back."

"I like you a little rounded."

She sniffed. "Right."

Carrying the baby, she walked to the sitting room, Dom on her heels.

"Sally says it will look better if I hold the baby while we're standing on the balcony, waving."

"Drat. I was hoping to do a Princess Kate and strategically place the blanket so no one can see I still have a baby bump."

Diaper bag over his shoulder, Dom held the apartment door open for her. "You're paranoid."

"Isabelle doesn't think so," she said, referring to the nanny who had just been hired by Sally. "She perfectly understands wanting to look my best in public."

They entered the elevator. Dom pressed the button for the second floor. When the doors opened, the king and Ginny's mom stood waiting for them.

Rose said, "I get to hold him first."

The king nudged her aside. "You held him first yesterday."

Bodyguards silently, expressionlessly stood by doors, glanced out windows.

Rose sighed. "Fine."

Ronaldo said, "Maybe I should be the one to hold him on the balcony."

Dom and Ginny simultaneously said, "No!"

"I need him and a long blanket to cover my baby weight."

"And Sally says my holding Jimmy will go a long way toward repairing my image for not being around for the baby's birth."

The king laughed as he led the three adults to his quarters. "You're a war hero."

Dom blew out his breath disgustedly. "Some war hero."

"Hey, you made the choice to call in the local police rather than send in the military. Technically, that was the big decision of the conflict."

Jimmy squirmed and began to whimper. Rose immediately took him from Ronaldo's arms. "Come to your Grammy Pajammy, sweet boy," she crooned, patting his back.

Dom said, "Grammy Pajammy?"

His father sighed. "It's a long story."

Ginny rolled her eyes. "I called her Mama Pajama until I was about ten."

Dom laughed. "Really?" Then he frowned and glanced at his dad. "And how do you know this?"

The king slid his arm around Rose's shoulders. "I suppose this is as good of a time as any to come clean about our relationship."

Ginny laughed but Dom's mouth fell open. "What?"

Rose grinned. "Second chance at love, honey." She leaned over the baby to put a kiss on the king's cheek. "There's nothing like it."

Dom stood shell-shocked, and Ginny held her breath. She'd suspected a little something was going on with her mom and the king, but buried in their own problems, neither she nor Dom had actually seen it.

Finally, Dom's lips lifted into a smile. His simple heartfelt "Welcome to the family" warmed Ginny all over. So did the realization that her mom would be staying. Forever.

She had a family.

They walked through two sitting rooms and a den to get to the balcony. Ginny put a blanket over her arm in such a way it draped in front of her stomach, and Rose placed the baby in her arms.

But right before they would have stepped out onto the balcony, she stopped and smiled at Dom. "Here."

"You're letting me hold him?"

"He's yours as well as mine." She sighed. "Besides, the bigger I look today the easier it will be for people to notice I'm losing weight."

He laughed and stepped out onto the balcony, but he stopped, too.

He caught his dad's gaze. "You and Rose come with us."

His dad waved a hand. "No. No. You and Ginny and Jimmy are the stars here. Have your moment in the sun."

"I'd rather we looked like a family."

Rose said, "Mmm-hmm."

Ginny pressed a finger to her lips to keep her still-humming hormones from making her cry. They hadn't had a big discussion about the king keeping Ginny's labor from Dom. When they'd returned the day before, Dom had simply said, "You were right," and King Ronaldo had nodded. Dom wanting them to be a family spoke volumes.

The king said, "I think that would be nice."

They stepped out onto the balcony to present their son to the kingdom and in the last second, Alex came racing through the door. "I heard this is a family moment."

Dom said, "It is."

Alex straightened to his full height, grinning like an idiot.

Ginny leaned over to Dom and whispered, "What's up with him?"

"Our father and Princess Eva's father are having a phone call tomorrow to talk about the wedding. He's trying to get on Dad's good side, hoping he'll give him another year of freedom."

Ginny winced. "Do you think your dad will do it?"

Dom glanced at his father, who beamed at little Jimmy and laughed. "Nope. I think my dad likes being a grandfather." He cuddled Jimmy to him, then waved to the crowd below.

Ginny nestled against him. "We'll give him another one soon."

Dom glanced down at her. "Really?"

Ginny laughed and snuggled more tightly against him. "Sure, we'll have two kids, and then I'll get my figure back, and then it's Alex and Eva's turn."

Cameras whirred and flashed, but Ginny didn't care. For twenty-five years she'd longed for a family and she'd finally gotten one.

* * * * *

MILLS & BOON®
Hardback – February 2016

ROMANCE

Leonetti's Housekeeper Bride	Lynne Graham
The Surprise De Angelis Baby	Cathy Williams
Castelli's Virgin Widow	Caitlin Crews
The Consequence He Must Claim	Dani Collins
Helios Crowns His Mistress	Michelle Smart
Illicit Night with the Greek	Susanna Carr
The Sheikh's Pregnant Prisoner	Tara Pammi
A Deal Sealed by Passion	Louise Fuller
Saved by the CEO	Barbara Wallace
Pregnant with a Royal Baby!	Susan Meier
A Deal to Mend Their Marriage	Michelle Douglas
Swept into the Rich Man's World	Katrina Cudmore
His Shock Valentine's Proposal	Amy Ruttan
Craving Her Ex-Army Doc	Amy Ruttan
The Man She Could Never Forget	Meredith Webber
The Nurse Who Stole His Heart	Alison Roberts
Her Holiday Miracle	Joanna Neil
Discovering Dr Riley	Annie Claydon
His Forever Family	Sarah M. Anderson
How to Sleep with the Boss	Janice Maynard

MILLS & BOON®
Large Print – February 2016

ROMANCE

Claimed for Makarov's Baby	Sharon Kendrick
An Heir Fit for a King	Abby Green
The Wedding Night Debt	Cathy Williams
Seducing His Enemy's Daughter	Annie West
Reunited for the Billionaire's Legacy	Jennifer Hayward
Hidden in the Sheikh's Harem	Michelle Conder
Resisting the Sicilian Playboy	Amanda Cinelli
Soldier, Hero...Husband?	Cara Colter
Falling for Mr December	Kate Hardy
The Baby Who Saved Christmas	Alison Roberts
A Proposal Worth Millions	Sophie Pembroke

HISTORICAL

Christian Seaton: Duke of Danger	Carole Mortimer
The Soldier's Rebel Lover	Marguerite Kaye
Return of Scandal's Son	Janice Preston
The Forgotten Daughter	Lauri Robinson
No Conventional Miss	Eleanor Webster

MEDICAL

Hot Doc from Her Past	Tina Beckett
Surgeons, Rivals...Lovers	Amalie Berlin
Best Friend to Perfect Bride	Jennifer Taylor
Resisting Her Rebel Doc	Joanna Neil
A Baby to Bind Them	Susanne Hampton
Doctor...to Duchess?	Annie O'Neil

MILLS & BOON®
Hardback – March 2016

ROMANCE

The Italian's Ruthless Seduction	Miranda Lee
Awakened by Her Desert Captor	Abby Green
A Forbidden Temptation	Anne Mather
A Vow to Secure His Legacy	Annie West
Carrying the King's Pride	Jennifer Hayward
Bound to the Tuscan Billionaire	Susan Stephens
Required to Wear the Tycoon's Ring	Maggie Cox
The Secret That Shocked De Santis	Natalie Anderson
The Greek's Ready-Made Wife	Jennifer Faye
Crown Prince's Chosen Bride	Kandy Shepherd
Billionaire, Boss...Bridegroom?	Kate Hardy
Married for their Miracle Baby	Soraya Lane
The Socialite's Secret	Carol Marinelli
London's Most Eligible Doctor	Annie O'Neil
Saving Maddie's Baby	Marion Lennox
A Sheikh to Capture Her Heart	Meredith Webber
Breaking All Their Rules	Sue MacKay
One Life-Changing Night	Louisa Heaton
The CEO's Unexpected Child	Andrea Laurence
Snowbound with the Boss	Maureen Child

MILLS & BOON®
Large Print – March 2016

ROMANCE

A Christmas Vow of Seduction	Maisey Yates
Brazilian's Nine Months' Notice	Susan Stephens
The Sheikh's Christmas Conquest	Sharon Kendrick
Shackled to the Sheikh	Trish Morey
Unwrapping the Castelli Secret	Caitlin Crews
A Marriage Fit for a Sinner	Maya Blake
Larenzo's Christmas Baby	Kate Hewitt
His Lost-and-Found Bride	Scarlet Wilson
Housekeeper Under the Mistletoe	Cara Colter
Gift-Wrapped in Her Wedding Dress	Kandy Shepherd
The Prince's Christmas Vow	Jennifer Faye

HISTORICAL

His Housekeeper's Christmas Wish	Louise Allen
Temptation of a Governess	Sarah Mallory
The Demure Miss Manning	Amanda McCabe
Enticing Benedict Cole	Eliza Redgold
In the King's Service	Margaret Moore

MEDICAL

Falling at the Surgeon's Feet	Lucy Ryder
One Night in New York	Amy Ruttan
Daredevil, Doctor...Husband?	Alison Roberts
The Doctor She'd Never Forget	Annie Claydon
Reunited...in Paris!	Sue MacKay
French Fling to Forever	Karin Baine

0216 GEN STD LP